# Creating Andy

*A light science fiction story
for Archaeology nerds.
A love and family story for all of us.*

*by*
*E. A. Owings*

*Illustrations by Morgan Coon*

# FACT OR FICTION?

Got questions about anything you read in this book?  Check the author's "CLAIMS AND DISCLAIMERS" on the last page.

# NOTE TO PARENTS

This science-fiction story makes frequent references to human reproduction, ranging from accidental to laboratory-assisted, including the terminology associated with those subjects.  The story also includes incidents of cloning and research involving embryonic cells.  Some characters face socially difficult situations including decisions regarding vasectomy and abortion.  A secondary character in the story is gay.

I believe that this story contains some valuable social messages for people of all ages.  However, due to the nature of the subject, I would suggest that parents use discretion in approving the book for anyone under the age of 17.

Sincerely,    E. A. Owings

# TABLE OF CONTENTS

# PROLOGUE

His name is Andy.

Or at least, that's the name he was accidentally given over 20 years ago. In fact, Andy's entire existence has been the result of a series of accidents, a fact that drove all of us nuts throughout most of the last two decades, but now seems too amazing to be anything but providential. Life is strange, and lives don't get much stranger than Andy's.

Not that there's anything too strange about being conceived unintentionally. It happens every day in bedrooms throughout the world and in the back seats of old Chevys, and it accounts for the existence of some of my best friends. Nor, in today's world, is there anything too strange about being conceived in a fertility lab. That, too, has led to the existence of some pretty amazing people, including Andy's older brother, Aiden, who makes the world a slightly kinder, gentler place.

But conception through a fertility lab is a carefully managed, time-consuming, and expensive process that doesn't generally happen by accident. That's what makes Andy different: he was both a remarkable fertility-lab achievement and a complete accident.

Oh, and there's one other teeny, weeny little thing that makes him different.

Genetically, he is 100% Neanderthal.

His name is Andy, and this is his story.

# PART 1: BEFORE

# CHAPTER 1: INTRODUCTIONS

I'm Larry Tanner, and my role in this whole amazing mess began over two decades ago in the spring of 2001 when Louis and I were archaeology graduate students at Pine State University. Aside from our shared interest in ancient humanity, my older brother and I are very different individuals starting with how we handle our names. Louis's name must always be pronounced LOO-iss, never LOO-ee, and I can almost hear him beginning to come unglued on the rare occasions when someone just shortens it to "Lou."

I'm just the opposite: "Lawrence" has always felt too formal for me, so I'm more comfortable with just being Larry. And Louis, in spite of his rigid rules about his own name, has no reservations about calling me "Larry Lamebrain," or "Lamebrain," or just "Lame." Of course, he didn't use any of those names in the presence of our parents, and I never made an issue of it when we were alone because I honestly didn't mind too much. I guess I had decided long ago that it was one of the unwritten privileges of older brotherhood. Plus, if he was calling me that name, then he was actually speaking to me, which I thought was freaking awesome.

Besides, Louis and I both knew where the realities of that nickname began and where they left off. The "lame" part of it definitely described my lifestyle, at least in comparison to Louis's. Brain-wise, my intellect could stand up to his any day. Louis is a smart guy, but my IQ tests actually scored a few points higher than his. It was what I *did* with my brain, and with every other aspect of my life, that left Louis and my parents shaking their heads.

Louis was, and still is, the studious type. Shy by nature, he seems happiest when he is immersed in his books or his laboratory work. I've sometimes jokingly called him the mad scientist, but there isn't really anything "mad" about him, with the glaring exception of the events that led up to this story. He is simply the most dedicated, diligent, and disciplined researcher that anyone could imagine.

I'm just the opposite, or at least I was back then. If there was fun to be had, I wasn't going to miss out on it. I skated through high school and my undergrad years by cramming for exams, which I usually aced much to Louis's frustration, and then blasting myself as far away from the world of academia as I could manage. Fortunately, Pine State U was surrounded by activities for its youthful Midwestern students, so I found it easy to access ski slopes in the winter, hiking trails in the spring and fall, or beach parties on the Lake Michigan shoreline in the summer. And, to be honest, it wasn't just the athletic challenges that I sought when I was off campus. I've always been a social animal. I can strum a pretty mean guitar, and the social atmosphere that Louis avoided so desperately was life-giving to me.

And, like most of the other guys in my dorm, I found those events to be most appealing if they included some of those amazing creations known as females, who could make Louis blush and plan a hasty exit just by their presence.

My parents weren't surprised when Louis chose Pine State University. He certainly had the qualifications to attend an Ivy League university, but Pine State offered him the things he wanted most: a private dorm room, his own little cubicle in the archaeology/anthropology building, and 24-hour access to the lab. It also was only about a two-hour drive from our parents' house, allowing him to go home on holidays and whenever else he felt like making the trip and eating some of Mom's cooking.

What did surprise our parents was when I decided to join Louis a year later. Frankly, I think they were a bit relieved that I was going to college at all. It hadn't looked promising on a Monday morning late in my senior year when my dad couldn't leave for work because his car wasn't in the driveway. Turned out it had been impounded when I, and several other classmates, got busted at a party where we weren't old enough to be consuming the beer that flowed freely.

I thought my father was going to have a coronary. He didn't say much, but the look of absolute rage on his red face made it clear that he was walking away only because anything he might have said or done at that moment probably would have gotten him into even deeper trouble than I had encountered. I really did feel awful about it, and after that I decided that my life of wine, women, and song needed to happen without the wine, or, in my case, the beer. From then on, and to this day, my recreational beverage became soda pop.

After that incident, it was clear that my parents weren't going to pay for me to go to college on the sunny beaches of California, so following Louis to Pine State made sense to me. I could have plenty of fun on the local slopes and beaches, and, besides, Louis's interest in archaeology had kind of rubbed off on me.

By the time we reached grad school, Louis and I had established a reputation throughout our region as budding experts on the subject of Neanderthals. Although I couldn't stand to spend quite as much time in the lab as Louis did, I knew my way around a genetic profile and could, when forced, analyze the content of a shard of bone just as well as he could. (Being brothers didn't prevent us from being competitive.) But my goal was to take a broader approach, analyzing the whole picture of Neanderthal cultures and comparing it to modern man. My studies were as much anthropology as archaeology. I wanted to understand the Neanderthal lifestyle; whether they had language, art, and music, and whether they were peaceful or warlike. From what we know so far, it appears that they lived in small family groups and generally avoided war.

In that aspect, they may have been ahead of our species.

# CHAPTER 2: THE EXPEDITION

It was our reputation as prominent students of
Neanderthal culture that bought us access to an
archaeological expedition to a mountainous region of
central Europe. Our flight left on March 17, 2001, the
first day of spring break. A part of me would rather
have been on a flight to Florida, partying with other
college students on the warm beaches, but I guess I had
matured a bit in the five years since Dad had to bail out
his car. So I really did find it interesting, if not truly
exciting, to be participating in an actual excavation
instead of analyzing bits of bone that someone else had
dug up years earlier. Besides, if nothing else, this
would be a change of scenery.

The scenery, though, turned out to be boringly
similar to what I saw in the landscapes near Pine State
U. Louis and I, along with a dozen other students, spent
the next day scraping and sifting rocky ground not far
from the shore of a freshwater lake, but we didn't find
much and the sun was hot. By late afternoon most of
the other students were ready for a break from the
beating sun and had begun to head back to their cabins.
Louis, however, wasn't quite ready to quit, and I was
more bored than tired, so I pointed to an area where
mountainous peaks shot up just a few miles from the
lake and convinced Louis to join me for a hike in the

cooler region. "Besides," I said, "Maybe the Neanderthals wanted to get away from the heat for a while, too. Maybe we'll find something interesting there."

Louis groaned, knowing that I was just making excuses, but he went along anyway. As the sun dipped low in the western sky, we drove our rental car as far up the mountain as possible and parked it in a small, empty parking area next to a weathered sign that read "Glacier Peaks." Then we picked up our backpacks and began hiking east toward two peaks on a low ridge. The south side of the first peak had vegetation growing on it, but as soon as we passed around the ridge to the north side, we found ourselves walking on a ledge on a bare face of the peak. Not far below us was a wide ravine where the snow and ice never completely melted, although the melting had increased recently due to warming climate conditions.

As we picked our way along the rocky ledge, Louis, who rarely walked anywhere except down campus corridors, slipped on the loose rocks and slid about 30 feet down the rocky slope into the icy ravine. For one awful moment, I feared that my recklessness had killed or permanently injured my only brother. Fortunately, from what I could see, Louis wasn't seriously injured, although his left ankle appeared to be sprained. He sat in the wet snow, grasping his ankle and wincing in pain as I hurried farther up the trail to a point where I could climb down to assist him.

However, when I arrived, Louis, still sitting in the snow, seemed to have almost forgotten his injured ankle. Instead, he was staring, transfixed, at a patch of melting snow beside him.

Right next to Louis, barely covered by the rapidly melting ice, lay a fully intact, perfectly preserved corpse of a Neanderthal man.

Stunned, I brushed away some of the snow for a closer look. Every aspect of this specimen was absolutely perfect, as if he had been frozen in this ice for only a few days instead of at least 40,000 years. But even if Louis and I had not arrived on that day, climate change was bringing an end to the Neanderthal's quiet repose in the ice. Parts of his left side were already protruding from the ice.

For a moment, Louis and I just sat there, brushing away more snow and staring back and forth at each other, dumbfounded at the discovery. The next thing I knew, I was dancing around in the snow, doing fist-pumps and celebrating our incredible luck. "Dude, we're gonna be famous!" I yelled to the echoing cliffs. But Louis just sat there in the snow, inches from the corpse, transfixed by this amazing specimen.

Both of us had been informed that if we discovered anything big or important, we were to notify the archaeology experts instead of trying to remove it ourselves. I reached for my phone, but Louis touched my arm to stop me. "Hold on a minute, Larry," he said. I knew this was serious, because even though I had led him on this crazy hike resulting in a sprained ankle, he hadn't referred to me as Lamebrain.

Still staring at the corpse and speaking barely above an awe-struck whisper, Louis explained that after the authorities were called in, he and I would lose access to the specimen. "We'll get our 15 minutes of fame for finding it, but then it will be locked up at some museum here in this country and we won't be able to touch it." Turning his face to me, Louis continued in an almost desperate tone of voice. "I've been working with dried-up bone fragments for six years, and now I'm staring at a gold mine of perfectly preserved cells. I want to take samples back to the lab with me."

To sneak samples from the specimen would be highly illegal, but I was learning that, when it came to his research, Louis sometimes made exceptions to his strait-laced standards. This was a once-in-a-lifetime find, and Louis wasn't going to walk away from it without cell samples. And if Mr. Play-By-The-Rules was willing to take a chance, who was I to argue?

So I picked up Louis's backpack and handed him the case containing his biopsy needles. He proceeded to withdraw imperceptibly tiny cores of cells from different parts of the specimen, completing his work within a few minutes. In a see-no-evil move that I had mastered in my earlier years, I took those few minutes to explore the rest of the ravine before walking up the ridge to find a signal for my flip-phone.

While we waited for the excavation experts, Louis and I constructed our plan. When the experts arrived, I stayed with them to chatter and take lots of photos. That suited my extroverted nature and also provided a distraction while Louis used his sprained ankle and wet clothing as an excuse to request an early ride back to our cabin. We both knew that the real reason for Louis's hasty exit was to get his samples back to the freezer in our cabin before they began to deteriorate.

As the corpse was removed from the glacier, I was able to legitimately scavenge a few hairs and bits of his flesh that remained stuck in the ice. These would serve as the official source of cells for our research papers. The university and the world would know that we had epidermal cells from the Neanderthal, but only Louis and I and a small circle within the archaeology department would know about the internal cells we had obtained with the biopsy needles.

~~~

Back at the university, as expected, Louis and I were surrounded by reporters, but we stuck with the Tanner brothers' plan: I took my comfortable place in the spotlight while Louis made excuses to retreat to the lab. At one point, the reporters asked me whether the Neanderthal specimen had been given a name. I told them that an official name would probably be issued by the home country where the corpse had been found, but since he had been found in a place called Glacier Peaks, Louis and I were just calling him Glacier Pete.

The reporters seemed comfortable enough with that, and Glacier Pete was all over the headlines and TV newscasts for the next few weeks.

A few evenings later I brought Louis a sandwich in the lab and asked him how the cell samples looked. He reported in somewhat hushed tones that the cells were amazing; that he had never expected the opportunity to work with anything so well-preserved. But Louis wasn't as joyful as I had expected. Instead, he was quietly obsessed. He wanted more. He wanted to culture the cells.

That would present a problem, since the cells, though well-preserved, were dead. At that time, the only way to culture the cells would be to extract DNA from the dead cells and inject it into an enucleated live egg. I was familiar with the process in theory but had never actually attempted it. Louis explained to me that he had done this once with the dried remains of an extinct lizard that he found in Mexico. He put DNA from the specimen into an enucleated egg from a similarly sized living lizard and was able to culture some cells for study.

"You cloned the lizard?" I asked Louis in disbelief.

"No, of course not," Louis replied emphatically, explaining that he only cloned *cell groups* from the lizard. "This isn't *Jurassic Park*," he said. "I'm not interested in raising lizards. I wouldn't want the responsibility for them, and I don't even like lizards.

13

Besides, I'd get into a whole lot of trouble for that, and I'm trying to build my reputation not destroy it."

I grinned and said that if it was me, I would have created the lizards. Louis gave me that look that said I was back into Lamebrain territory.

Lizards aside, we both understood that procuring a human egg isn't as easy as digging up a lizard egg. The immature human eggs, or oocytes, that would be used for this type of project are microscopic and remain firmly lodged inside human females until they dissolve or are fertilized. They can be extracted in a fertility lab, but that option wasn't even remotely available to us. Or so it seemed.

# CHAPTER 3: EMILIE AND THE CLINIC

Archaeology and anthropology students were not the only university staff members who needed access to a genetics lab. In fact, we weren't even near the top of the list. The well-being of living humans was also at stake, so the state-of-the-art genetics lab at Pine State was actually a central hub surrounded by several departments in the human medical field studying genetic diseases and cellular abnormalities. Teams of experts examined cancerous cells, as well as cystic fibrosis, Huntington's disease, Klinefelter, Turner, and two kinds of Trisomy, to name a few.

Until I met Emilie, I hadn't even been aware that at the opposite end of this bustling hub was the university's reproductive clinic where couples struggling with infertility traveled for hundreds of miles to visit the renowned Dr. Tremblay.

Some of the professors at the university were very informal, even inviting their grad students to refer to them by their first names, but if Dr. Tremblay had a first name, almost nobody was aware of it. The rotund, white-haired 60-year-old doctor approached his clients with the deepest of compassion, but to his staff members he had all the warmth of a platoon sergeant. He ran a highly regimented organization, and he did so for good reasons: lives were at stake, or at least the quality of those lives, ranging from potential parents to potential children. Dr. Tremblay took them all seriously, and that meant that organization and perfection were essential. Any breach of protocols could ruin the reputation of his clinic, and even the slightest temperature variations in the freezers where sperm or embryos were stored could spell potential disaster. The university electricians and maintenance crew were instructed to answer his calls immediately, and his staff members were hired for their organizational skills and adherence to strict protocols.

Dr. Tremblay did have a small number of graduate students studying under him, but only because the university required it. As much as possible, he delegated those students to the lab where they could test for genetic abnormalities while staying out of his precious reproductive clinic.

It was in the genetics lab that I met Emilie. Did I mention my attraction to the females of our species? As an undergrad, I had done my share of partying, but since I had joined Louis in our graduate studies, and especially as he raced to conclude his Master's thesis, I had gradually joined him in the windowless life of the student lab-rat. Plus, of course, the whole Neanderthal incident had disrupted everything, so social activities had taken a distant back seat to responsibilities. One look at Emilie, though, and I envisioned a different type of back seat.

Through her work in the genetics lab, I had no doubt about Emilie's brain power, but at that time I was more attracted to the thick, dark hair, deep brown eyes, and delicate face that encased that wonderful cranium. Her family lived in Quebec, so I was also fascinated by her ability to speak French, a language I had never attempted to learn, since I have enough trouble with English. She was actually a year ahead of me in her studies, so she was scheduled to graduate at the same time as Louis, and she planned to accept an offer in Paris after graduation.

I sat beside Emilie a few times as she chatted in French with her mother on the phone, and found myself captivated by her voice. It was after one of those conversations that I found out why she was a student at Pine State. It turned out that Dr. Tremblay was her uncle, and she was actually living in a small apartment that had originally been a servant's quarters at the back of his heritage house. Her apartment had its own entrance, affording us a degree of privacy and freedom that would not have been possible had she been living in a dormitory.

During one of our conversations in her apartment, I learned more about Emilie's academic situation. Her uncle, as I've mentioned, was chief medical officer of the reproductive clinic, and Emilie was both his student and his teacher. She could converse with him about cellular development on a level that left me wondering whether they were speaking in French again.

But Emilie could do one thing that Dr. Tremblay would never be able to do. As a female, she could serve as a source of eggs for study.

Withdrawing eggs from women is an everyday process in a fertility clinic. The female patient is given hormones to cause the ovaries to release a number of eggs, and then the doctor removes them through microsurgery for in vitro fertilization. This has been done for decades and has been the source of countless successful pregnancies. But the eggs that Dr. Tremblay removed from his clients were held as sacred, for that woman's use only. Withdrawing eggs for study is a bit more controversial, so Dr. Tremblay was quietly elated to have a female relative who was as interested as he was in analyzing those eggs. Since her arrival at the college three years earlier, Emilie had produced nearly three dozen ova and oocytes for analysis, and she knew how to perform all kinds of experiments with them.

If such experimentation sounds a bit Frankenstein-ish, it's not, although it's mostly practiced in animals. Nuclear replacement is a regular practice for creating breeding stock in the livestock industry. Emilie and Dr. Tremblay knew how to enucleate her oocytes and test them in a variety of ways, but they were strictly examining zygotes of only a few cells, all of which were carefully incinerated after the data had been collected. Emilie, like Louis, wasn't creating any lizards.

Only a Lamebrain would do that.

# CHAPTER 4: WHILE THE CAT'S AWAY

For me, the gears were turning. In between enjoying Emilie's sweet voice and soft skin, I took the time to learn everything I could from her about how to enucleate an oocyte and insert alternate DNA into it. Emilie and I actually reached the point where we were spending more time in the lab than in her apartment. Finally, at almost the same time, we both spoke up and revealed that we wanted something, something very secret and academically inappropriate, from each other. But just as we were deciding that our plans weren't realistic, something unexpected happened.

Dr. Tremblay had spent decades paying more attention to the well-being of his patients and his clinic than his own health, and it finally caught up with him. Emilie called me one afternoon to inform me that her uncle had collapsed in the clinic hallway and had been transported by ambulance to the local hospital. I asked whether she wanted me to visit her there, but she said no. She would stay at his side until a diagnosis had been reached, and she would keep me posted by phone. Two days later, she called to inform me that he was expected to survive, but he would require major surgery to remove a portion of his intestine. He would be away from the clinic for at least six weeks, which meant being away from his students and clients for what little was left of the school year.

In Dr. Tremblay's absence, the clinic continued to function, but silent panic set in among his staff members. Since Emilie's position was in the lab rather than the clinic, she wasn't responsible for seeing patients, but those who had to do so were running themselves ragged, and a few grad students had been permitted to assist as desk clerks. Non-essential appointments were cancelled, but patients whose procedures had already been scheduled had to be seen with or without the good doctor's presence. Fortunately, some of his staff members knew how to conduct the usual procedures, but they were under a great deal of pressure and were generally exhausted by the end of the day.

With fewer patients on the schedule, Emilie's clinic-related lab work was actually reduced, giving her more time for her own lab work, and more time for me. We were able to resume our conversation about our secret projects.

Emilie had conducted tests on every type of genetic abnormality available to her, but she wanted to add one more thing to her thesis presentation: an in vitro study of an ovum being fertilized by a sperm and transforming into the early embryonic blastula stage. She wanted to film the process in real time and add it as a final dramatic ending to her thesis. From me, the only requirements would be providing a sperm sample and granting permission to destroy the embryo after filming, which her uncle would never have permitted if a client's embryo had been involved. I was willing on both counts.

What I wanted from her was a bit more complex. Did she have any of her frozen eggs left? Yes, a few. Did she have plans for them? No, they were destined for the incinerator. Would she help me insert Neanderthal DNA into one of those eggs so that I could provide some growing cell lines for Louis's studies? She said yes, on two conditions: First, I had to wait a few days until her project was completed and submitted. Second, I had to promise to stop at cell lines. No lizards, and no Neanderthals. I had no problem agreeing to this. Besides, human beings can't be grown in laboratory dishes. I couldn't create a person, Neanderthal or otherwise, unless the embryo was implanted in a female, and that, I said with a laugh, is not the sort of thing that happens accidentally.

# CHAPTER 5: IT'S A BLAST!

Watching Emilie's egg-fertilization video was fascinating. I had seen similar videos before, but not in real time, and certainly not involving *my* sperm. The realization that I could actually reproduce, not just in theory but in real life, was amazing to me. But now was not the time or the place for that reproduction, so, as planned, the microscopic blastula went into the incinerator. I waved goodbye to it, but any slight sense of loss was overshadowed by the science, as well as the potential, that I was observing. Besides, it was a small price to pay for my next project.

Now it was time to implement *my* plan. Emilie had three frozen oocytes that she agreed to let me use for my Neanderthal cell lines. With her help, I enucleated all of them and carefully inserted DNA that Louis had extracted from his Neanderthal cells. Then we watched. Activity, if it was going to happen, would occur within hours. As the minutes ticked by, we watched through the microscope camera as two of the eggs deteriorated. Just as we were about to give up, the third one began to show signs of activity: first, a quiver, then a hesitant cell division, and suddenly an explosion of activity.

We had a blastula!  A wonderful, amazing, indisputably growing embryo that had multiplied past 32 cells and reached the blastula stage.

Emilie cautioned me that I needed to act quickly.  Without wasting any time, I extracted a few stem cells from the blastula before those cells could begin differentiating.  If done properly, the blastula would recover, and more stem cells could be extracted at a later time.  As I watched the extracted cells dividing, Emilie placed the embryo back into the deep freeze.  I barely paid attention to what she was doing.  I couldn't take my eyes off of the stem cells that I had in front of me.  I rushed them off to Louis's cubicle, where he stared for only a moment before beginning his work.  He didn't ask how I got them.  He certainly knew, but he didn't want to know the details, and he didn't care.

In joy and relief, I returned to Emilie in the lab.  As usual, I couldn't stop talking, but Emilie was surprisingly quiet.  Finally, she said, "This embryo isn't going to last very long in this freezer."

"Why not?" I asked.

"This freezer is designed for storing dead cells," she replied.  "It doesn't have the finely-tuned temperature controls that we have in the freezers at the fertility lab."

Then she gave me a quick kiss, and she left.  Did she also give me a wink and a grin?  It seemed to me that she did, but I couldn't be sure.  Either way, my options were clear to me.  Emilie certainly could not give me permission to use the clinic freezer, but since Dr. Tremblay had gone to the hospital, she had given me a tour of the clinic, so I knew where the freezer was located. I also knew that in his absence, security wasn't up to his usual standards. I found the door from the genetics lab to the fertility clinic unlocked. Had someone forgotten to lock it, or had Emilie intentionally unlocked it for me? Again, I didn't know, and I didn't ask. I only knew that I had watched those stem cells divide, and I wasn't about to intentionally let my newly formed creation disintegrate now. At least, not until I was certain that Louis had extracted as many cells as he wanted from it.

The clinic staff members had gone home, so I made my way down the dim hallways to the freezer. Although the outside of the freezer was quite large, the temperature-controlled interior was surprisingly small due to the thick insulation surrounding it. Behind the glass doors inside, I saw racks containing a small number of vials identical to the one in which my quick-frozen embryo now rested. That was when I noticed that the vial I was holding was different from the ones at my lab station. It was even a different color. Emilie must have brought it with her from the clinic. Was this another silent signal that she was allowing me to use the freezer, or had she grabbed a clinic vial simply because she had a supply of them? Again, I didn't know, and it didn't really matter. I opened the glass door and placed the vial as far away from the other vials as I could. It wasn't very difficult to separate them. With Dr. Tremblay away, there were very few vials in storage, so there was plenty of room. I quickly closed the door before the temperature could rise enough to trigger an alarm, which would have not only foiled my plan but undoubtedly gotten me into deeper trouble than I wanted to imagine.

After closing the freezer door, I saw a sign saying that any unlabeled or improperly labeled vials would be discarded. Next to it was a sheet of blank labels, with only one label remaining on the sheet. Yes, of course, my vial would have to be labeled, but what should I write on it? Certainly not my name unless I wanted to sign my own arrest warrant, and certainly not Emilie's name unless I wanted to sign my own death warrant. The vial needed a name uniquely its own.

"Let's see," I thought. "Neanderthal?" No, that would get it thrown out in a hurry. But I needed a name that I could remember, and I wasn't in a position to write notes to myself at that moment. The sound of footsteps outside of the clinic was starting to make me nervous.

"NEEEEE ANNNDERRR..." I mumbled, knowing that I was wasting precious time and needed to get this figured out before someone discovered me in the clinic. But sheer terror had driven my mind back to Lamebrain status, and I wasn't coming up with anything original.

"NEEEEE..." Okay, I decided on the name, "Neil." That should work. It was normal enough not to draw too much attention to the vial. With trembling fingers, I wrote it in the first line. Next name: "ANNNDERRR..." Still drawing blanks, I decided on the name "Anderson." Okay, my embryo would be named "Neil Anderson." I kind of liked that. But before I could write that second name on the blank, I realized that the blanks were labeled, "Last name first."

Oh, crap. So "Neil" was already written in as the last name? Okay, that would still be workable. But I'd not yet heard of Anderson Cooper at that time, so "Anderson" didn't seem like a realistic first name. I shortened it to "Andrew" and filled in the blank for "sex." For "date collected," I chose a date just before Dr. Tremblay left, since anything later than that might look suspicious. Then I stuck the labeled vial back into the freezer and hurried out of the clinic.

When I sat down at my desk in the lab, I felt a sense of relief, a sense of accomplishment, and a little sense of that devious victory that I remembered from sneaking out to parties in my younger years. My project had a name now. It was Andrew, and it would be waiting for me in the clinic freezer whenever I wanted more stem cells from it.

Life was good.

# CHAPTER 6: ALICIA & ARNIE

It was early morning on the Friday before Memorial Day, and most classes had already been completed for the term. With few students left on campus, I enjoyed the scent of spring flowers as I walked from Emilie's apartment back to my dorm room. My walk took me past the front of the reproductive clinic, where a heavily-loaded minivan was just backing into a parking space near the entrance.

A woman stepped out of the passenger side of the mini-van, her blond hair tumbling around the shoulders of her sun dress as she closed the door.

"I'll probably only be a minute," she said to her husband, sitting in the driver's seat. He nodded and rolled the van windows down to let in some fresh air for himself, their 2-year-old son, and their Golden Retriever. The van was so densely packed with vacation supplies that he might not have been able to open any doors without something falling out.

I nodded and smiled at the man in the driver's seat, and then continued on my walk. I had never met these people before, and I never expected to meet them again, an assumption that turned out to be very, very wrong. I didn't see what happened when the woman entered the clinic, but I heard every detail of it a few days later from clinic staff members, and again months later when the woman herself told me all about it.

Inside the clinic, the blond-haired woman was surprised to see how empty the waiting room was. She had been here before, and there had always been at least a few women waiting, but today there was no one. She approached the desk, where she found an assistant whose name tag read "Linda P" shuffling through some paperwork.

"Good morning!" said Linda P., looking a bit surprised to see anyone. "What can I do for you today?"

"Probably nothing," answered the blond-haired woman. "Dr. Tremblay withdrew some eggs from me and told me that he would let me know if any of them developed into embryos after he injected them with Arnie's sperm. I'm at the right stage for implant now, but I haven't heard anything from Dr. Tremblay, so I'm assuming that none of the embryos survived. The last I heard from him, he said that it wasn't looking good, which was no surprise, really. We had to try IVF several times before we conceived Aiden, and I'm 34 years old now, so I'm not very optimistic."

Linda P. explained to her about Dr. Tremblay's hospitalization and apologized for the fact that she had not been notified. "I don't remember the doctor saying that he had any embryos for you, so you may be right about the outcome, but I can't say anything for certain right now. Let me check the computer. What is your name, ma'am?"

"Alicia Marie Neill," she answered.

"I see your file, and the date on which the eggs were extracted, but I'm not finding anything about embryos available for transplant," said Linda P. "But your extraction was done just before Dr. Tremblay was hospitalized, so I can't be sure whether the failure was in the embryos or the records. Let me send someone back to check the freezer."

A few minutes later, Linda P. was called to the back room by two other clinic staff members with baffled looks on their faces. "We're not sure what to make of this, but this is what we found in the freezer," said a staff member named Carol, displaying a digital photograph of a label.

"The name is rather sloppily written, and it says, 'Neil, Andrew,' continued Carol. "But our client's name is Alicia, and her husband's name is Arnold, not Andrew, and her last name is spelled with two Ls, not one."

Linda P. sat down at a computer terminal in the back room and brought up Alicia's file. "Well, our records show that the client's maiden name was 'Andrews,' so maybe that's why someone wrote it that way? Some women do hyphenate their names, but I don't think Mrs. Neill does, and she's an established client here. She didn't hyphenate her name when she conceived her first child, so I don't know why anyone would think she'd hyphenate it this time."

Carol replied, "I'm not sure either, but that was three years ago, and some of our staff haven't been here that long. What baffles me is that anyone here would be so careless in their labeling. Dr. Tremblay would have conniption fits if he saw this label."

Then she added, "Nevertheless, I suppose we'd better call and ask him about it."

"Unfortunately, we can't," answered Linda P. as she continued to search through the computer records. "Not today anyway. Part of his intestinal surgery didn't go as planned the first time, so he's back in surgery today. They're probably prepping him for surgery as we speak."

"But I can't find any evidence that it could belong to anyone else," Linda continued. "We have no other clients named Neil, with either one L or two, and no clients at all named Andrew or Andrews or Anders or Anderson or anything like that.

"Furthermore, the extraction date matches hers, and we had no other extractions on that date. Dr. Tremblay got sick later that same day, so we had no other extractions that entire week. I just don't see how it could belong to anyone else. Just by a process of elimination, it has to be hers," concluded Linda P.

"We had a couple of grad students working that week who were more concerned about their exams than their work," added Carol. "And we can't ask them about it, either, because they've gone home for the summer."

Linda P. took a deep breath and said, "Okay, I'll handle this." She walked back to the lobby and showed the label photo to Mrs. Neill.

"We apologize for the labeling, but our records indicate that this must be your embryo," she told Alicia, adding, "If you'd like, you can come back next month."

"No, we're leaving today for our summer vacation. Arnie is waiting in the car with our son Aiden and our dog, Gus," replied Alicia. Changing the subject, she asked, "What do we know about the embryo? Does it look good? Do we know whether it's male or female?"

"It looks excellent," replied Linda P. "And the label says it's male."

"Well, Aiden would love a little brother," said Alicia, trying to force her mind back to the important issue at hand.

Finally she concluded, "Well, it appears to be just a labeling issue, which isn't too surprising when students are involved. With Dr. Tremblay gone, there just wasn't the oversight that normally would have occurred. So, if you're sure it's mine..."

"It definitely doesn't belong to any of our other clients," answered Linda P. "I checked and double-checked that. And we don't store embryos for other clinics."

Alicia had entered the clinic fully prepared to accept the fact that even with IVF, she would probably never be able to get pregnant again. Now, suddenly, she felt the overwhelming joy of realizing that a second baby was a very clear possibility.

"Well, let's get this done so I can leave for my vacation!" she exclaimed. Linda P. and the others spun around and headed for their positions in the exam room. Alicia stepped outside to tell Arnie that it might be a while, but he had already taken Aiden and Gus out of the van and was walking around the commons with them. She returned to the exam room and put her feet in the stirrups, still trembling with excitement.

After the procedure had been completed and Alicia was checking out at the desk, Linda P. said, "Be sure to check in with us in four-to-six weeks so we can do a pregnancy test."

"Oh, I won't be here in four-to-six weeks," answered Alicia. "Arnie and I are teachers, so our summer vacation is just beginning, and we're heading up to Canada for the entire summer. My dad owns five acres with three cabins on a river in northern Ontario, and we spend as much time as possible there during the summer months. My brother and his wife will be up there, too, and they have two daughters around Aiden's age, so they'll all have a great time. We'll be fishing and swimming and sitting around the fireside in the evenings. I'm really looking forward to de-stressing. We'll be off-line and off-grid for the entire summer.

"But don't worry... if I get pregnant, I'll know," added Alicia with a grin. "This isn't my first pregnancy."

Linda P. nodded and rolled her chair to a cabinet behind her. "Okay, but you'd better take some supplies with you," she said. She put three pregnancy tests and a 90-day supply of prenatal vitamins into a plastic bag, and then tossed in an old stethoscope that had been left on top of the filing cabinet. Handing it to Alicia, she said, "And check in with us when you get back!"

"Will do!" replied Alicia as she stared at the contents of the bag, still processing what had happened within the last few minutes.

Linda P. smiled and said, "If the implanted embryo develops, do you know what you plan to name the baby?"

"Judging from that strange label, I'd say he already has a name," laughed Alicia. "His name seems to be Andrew, which actually works fine for us. Names beginning with "A" seem to be a trademark of our family: Arnie, Alicia, Aiden, and now, just maybe, Andrew. I think I like that." Then she waved and walked out the front door.

Linda P. watched through the front window as Alicia met up with Arnie on the front lawn, exchanged a quick kiss with him, loaded Aiden and Gus back into the van, and rolled off toward the Mackinac Bridge.

# **CHAPTER 7: THE AFTERMATH**

I have never in my life, either before or in the 20+ years since this incident, experienced the level of sheer terror that I felt on the day we discovered that the Neanderthal embryo was missing. I felt as if all the blood had been drained out of me and as if I might vomit at any moment. Emilie was furious, and Louis just held his head in his hands as if he couldn't believe this was happening. Both Louis and Emilie had been presented with their Masters Degrees just days earlier, and if their role in this mess was discovered, it was likely that both degrees would be revoked by the university.

I had spent most of my life evading responsibility, but I suddenly came to the conclusion that all of that would come to an end right now. No one else knew about the Neanderthal embryo yet, but as soon as Dr. Tremblay recovered from his surgery, he would undoubtedly confirm that the embryo in the vial did not belong to Mrs. Neill, and the proverbial excrement would hit the fan. Yes, I would be expelled from the university. That was an absolute certainty. It was also quite possible that I would face civil and criminal charges. But, as I stopped to breathe for a moment, I realized that I would probably survive all of it. What I had done was awful, but I probably wasn't going to be drawn and quartered, or fed to the lions, so, at some point, I would get my life back, or at least some portion of it. I might be flipping burgers for the rest of my life, but at least I would have a life.

What was most important to me at this point was protecting Emilie and Louis. They had played only minor roles in this mess anyway, and those roles did not need to be revealed. My only option was to take full responsibility for my actions and insist that I acted alone. I would tell the administration that I stole Emilie's oocytes from the freezer and that it was entirely my idea to grow cell lines from Glacier Pete. I would lie under oath if necessary. At this point, implicating Louis and Emilie would do nothing to save me and would do everything to ruin them.

I made that promise to both of them as I helped Emilie carry her suitcases to her car. She planned to head back to Quebec briefly and then leave as quickly as possible for her new job in Paris. As she stepped into her car, I asked her whether I would see her again. She said nothing, but glared at me in a way that clearly said if I ever stepped within a hundred yards of her, she would call the police. Fair enough. I respected her wishes and never saw her again, except for a brief moment 18 years later. I did see her name throughout the next few years in research reports from Paris, so I know that she was successful in her career. It was the best outcome I could have expected under the circumstances.

That night I sat down at my computer and composed a letter explaining everything that I had done, minus any implication of Louis or Emilie. I printed three copies, which I submitted the next day to the head of the archaeology department, the Dean of Student Affairs, and, of course, the reproductive clinic. I dropped off the latter copy at the clinic rather than directly to Dr. Tremblay, leaving his staff in the unfortunate position of deciding when they could inform the doctor without further endangering his health. The other two letters I delivered by hand so that I could personally express my remorse. Of course, I also offered to do anything in my power to rectify the situation, but as expected, the administration only wanted me out of there as quickly as possible.

The Dean of Student Affairs (DSA) was particularly annoyed to be dealing with this mess because he was just in the process of moving his family to a newer house the university had provided for them. The last thing he wanted was to have to deal with more meetings, more hearings, and more controversy. I had wasted enough of his time when Louis and I discovered Glacier Pete, and now this.

As expected, my expulsion papers arrived by registered mail the next day. I felt an awful knot in the pit of my stomach when I held those papers in my hand, but it wasn't a surprise, and I also felt some sense of relief that it was over, at least for now.

As it turned out, I didn't need to do any extensive lying to avoid implicating Emilie or Louis. The university administration definitely wanted my hide, but they seemed quite willing to accept that I had acted alone. Emilie was in France, which made it difficult to question her, and the university didn't want to alienate Dr. Tremblay by pursuing her internationally. And Louis was a respected researcher who had brought some degree of fame to the university with his analysis of Glacier Pete, so they weren't really eager to stain his name, either. Besides, when it came down to the facts, the university didn't really have a shred of evidence against either of them, so pursuing charges would probably have been a wasted effort. However, they must have suspected that Louis was at least aware of my activities, because they quietly denied his application to do his doctoral studies at Pine State. Louis didn't seem too upset about that, as other universities would be eager to accept him, but Pine State had been his home for six years and he would miss it.

Louis and I didn't have much to say as we drove back to our parents' house the next day. I watched lilac bushes and flowering dogwood trees alongside the road as we left the university expecting never to see the campus again.

# CHAPTER 8: ALICIA RETURNS

During my association with Emilie, I had gotten to know a few of the staff members at the fertility clinic, and they kept me somewhat updated on what happened over the summer months. As expected, a flurry of administrative meetings ensued. Dr. Tremblay returned from his sick bed long enough to raise hell with his staff for allowing such a thing to happen, and to explain to the administrators that an implanted embryo does not always result in a pregnancy. Every effort was made to contact Alicia Neill, but she had been serious when she said that she would be off-line and off-grid for the entire summer and that most of her family would be with her. All attempts to contact her failed. The university administrators would have no choice but to wait.

As Alicia told me later, she returned from Canada on Labor Day weekend and just left a message on the clinic's overnight answering machine saying that she was happily pregnant and was available to schedule an appointment at the clinic's earliest convenience. At that point, she was just following up on the instructions that she had been given when she left in May. She was surprised when the clinic called the next morning and said that they wanted to see her immediately and that she should bring her husband with her. Why on earth would Arnie need to be there to confirm a pregnancy that he already knew about?  And she hadn't yet been to the clinic for an ultrasound, so it didn't seem likely that the clinic would know about any fetal abnormalities yet.  None of it made any sense to her. She scheduled an appointment for 1:15 p.m. and was told not to eat anything before her arrival.  She told the clinic staff that Arnie, who was the high school's assistant athletic director, was busy getting his sports programs set up and would not be able to attend.  She dropped off Aiden at her parents' house and arrived at the clinic alone.

Alicia had expected to be ushered into the examining room, but instead she was escorted to a small conference room where she found herself across the table from several somber-faced administrators and, of course, Dr. Tremblay, who looked as if he wished he could be back in the hospital getting some more of his intestines removed.

The administrators explained everything as briefly and sympathetically as possible.  They told her that a now-expelled student (me, of course) had been responsible for this atrocity and would be punished to the fullest extent of the law.  For now, the university and the clinic could only extend their sincere apologies and correct the problem as quickly as possible.  They told her that the examining room was already set up for a prompt and relatively painless termination of this unfortunate pregnancy.  In a move that struck her as just a bit too contrived and condescending, they opened the conference room door and gestured toward the room at the end of the hall.

But Alicia Neill wasn't quite so easily convinced. As a high school teacher, she had faced down administrators, parents, and every type of manipulative student too many times to be easily intimidated. She had learned that if she was being pressured into a decision that she wasn't ready to make, there was almost always one other option.

"I'll get back to you on that," she said, with a fiery determination in her eyes that intimidated all but one of the administrators.

"Of course," said that last guy. "But it wouldn't be a good idea to postpone the inevitable for very long. You would be doing yourself no favor by prolonging the development of a severely abnormal fetus."

"I said I'd get back to you!" snapped Alicia in a tone that even the tough guy couldn't ignore this time. Then she walked out the front door and took a deep breath.

There was a bench about 60 feet out from the front door of the clinic, and Alicia stopped there to compose herself. The impact of the news hit her, and she fought back tears. Thirteen weeks ago, she had convinced herself that the embryo in the vial belonged to her and Arnie, and together they had reveled in that news. They had celebrated the positive pregnancy tests, and they had listened to the tiny heartbeat. It had seemed too good to be true, and it was. Now she was being told that the fetus she was carrying not only wasn't hers but wasn't even human. Well, not modern human anyway. It was a nightmare, and she only wished that she would wake up from it.

"Mrs. Neill?" I said.

Alicia looked up, startled. She had been so lost in her thoughts that she hadn't seen me approaching her. But my appearance was no accident. Sources at the clinic had informed me of Alicia's upcoming appointment, so Louis and I had borrowed our dad's pickup truck and 5th wheel camper and found a campsite outside of the college town. I was persona-non-grata on campus, so I had known better than to step foot inside the clinic, but I had managed to park the truck in the front lot to wait for her. Louis waited in the truck.

I sat on the other end of the bench and explained who I was. I apologized for my role in the creation of the embryo, and emphasized that I had never intended for it to be implanted in anyone. She nodded numbly. She had been hearing apologies all morning and they had become meaningless.

I had written my name and cellphone number on a slip of paper, which I handed to her. "If there is anything I can do for you, any information I can provide or any help I can offer, just call," I said. "Any time, day or night. I mean that literally."

"Thank you," she replied, "but I don't know how you could help."

"Neither do I, except that my brother and I may still be your best local source of information about Neanderthals," I explained. "Louis has been studying them for six years, and I've been studying them for five. I guess you know that we discovered and examined Glacier Pete, who was Andy's clone," I said.

"Andy?" she asked.

"Oh, I'm sorry. That's the name I gave the embryo when I put it in the freezer," I explained. "I presume you've given him a different name, if you've named him at all." I had the feeling that I was digging myself a deep hole, but Alicia didn't seem offended.

"No, actually, that's what we've been calling him, too," she said with a tone of relief in her voice. It was the first time all morning that anyone had addressed the humanity, or near humanity, or potential humanity, of her pregnancy. She accepted the slip of paper with my phone number on it, and started to walk toward her car. But after only a few steps she stopped, turned around, and walked back into the clinic.

I wondered whether she had decided to terminate the pregnancy, as the university administrators had recommended. Desperate to know for sure, I texted my source in the fertility clinic and waited agonizing minutes for the answer. Finally, it came: No. Alicia had walked into the clinic and demanded an ultrasound. She wanted to know whether her fetus had any abnormalities besides being Neanderthal. I couldn't help chuckling a bit. Any abnormalities **besides** being

Neanderthal?  But it actually made sense.  Alicia was a teacher.  She was dedicated to finding answers, and she was going to go into this decision with as many facts in front of her as possible.  And the clinic staff, at least the ones not associated with the administration, were dedicated to helping her do just that.

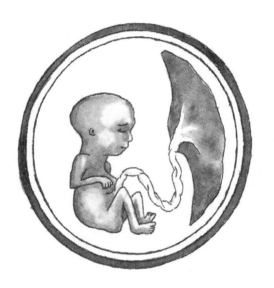

# CHAPTER 9: JUST THE FACTS, MA'AM

Just a few days before Alicia Neill's visit to the clinic, she had been thrilled to feel the first flutter of movement in her lower abdomen. Now she needed to know as much as possible about Whatever-It-Was that was fluttering around in there.

The ultrasound technician was prepared for this. Although the university and clinic administrators had been determined to make this pregnancy go away, the clinic staff had been quietly preparing for other possibilities. As the technician showed Alicia the images on the screen, she confided to Alicia that she and the other staff members had secretly consulted with me and Louis, as well as any other sources they could find, about what to expect from a developing Neanderthal. A normal *Homo sapiens* fetus at 13 weeks would be about the size of a lemon. Andy was slightly larger, with a more robust skeleton and a skull that was slightly longer from front to back.

"That's normal, from what I've learned," said the technician. "His brain, at birth, would be the same size as a modern human brain, but the skull would be a bit larger and would grow rapidly in the first few months after birth to accommodate the larger brain."

"Larger brain?" asked Alicia. "Neanderthals actually had *larger* brains than we do?"

"Apparently so," answered the technician.

"How would that affect the birth?" asked Alicia. "Is that large skull going to fit through the birth canal?"

"I'm told that Neanderthal women had slightly larger pelvic openings. If you give birth to this baby, you might need to consider a C-section."

That wasn't what Alicia wanted to hear, but she continued to watch the image on the screen, comparing it, as well as she could remember, to the images that she had seen during Aiden's development. This fetus was definitely huskier, but otherwise not much different. And he was very active. It seemed that these procedures had disturbed his sleep, and he was rearranging himself for a more comfortable position.

Alicia thanked the technician and left. She drove to her parents' house to pick up Aiden, and explained to them that she might need to drop him off again in the next couple of days because there were some possible complications to her pregnancy. They agreed, and she chose not to go into any more detail at this time. She took Aiden to the local playground, partly to clear her mind and partly to let him use up plenty of energy so that he would get to sleep at a reasonable hour. She knew that she would need time to think and time to talk with Arnie.

As she pushed Aiden on the swing, Alicia considered her options. As a high school teacher, she had seen many girls get pregnant, sometimes under the most horrendous circumstances. And as a woman in her mid-30s, she had seen other adult women confronted with pregnancies that had been much wanted but had gone horribly wrong. With all of that in mind, she wasn't opposed to terminating pregnancies, and she needed to consider the reasons why it might be the best (or the only) option in this situation. She could see that the university administrators were pushing it for THEIR reasons, which she had every right to reject. But what about HER reasons? And Arnie's? And maybe even Aiden's? How would this affect their lives? And what about Andy himself? At this point, he was just developing as a Neanderthal fetus should, but what type of world would he be entering? Would he be able to cope with modern surroundings? Would he spend his life as a freak to be ridiculed? Would he even survive the viruses and bacteria and contaminants that his species had never encountered? She needed answers, and she needed them soon.

Arnie had been informed that there was a problem with the pregnancy, but Alicia waited until Aiden was asleep to discuss it with him. Then she waited while he worked his way through the shock, anger, and disappointment that she had experienced hours earlier.

It was 9 p.m. when they called me.

# CHAPTER 10: PREDICTIONS

Louis and I arrived at the Neill home within 20 minutes. We had been preparing for this moment for months (and unknowingly for years) so we had stacks of paperwork with us, as well as a laptop computer filled with statistics and images from our research.

Of course, we had photos of Glacier Pete, who, as Andy's clone, would be nearly identical in appearance. But those pictures weren't very appealing to someone trying to determine the future of a baby. Glacier Pete, by archaeology standards, was remarkably well preserved, but he was also hairy, battered, discolored, and, of course, very dead. Alicia looked at the pictures and grimaced.

When it came to the questions that Alicia and Arnie had, we were forced to admit that our answers would be mostly speculative, although we did have some evidence to back up our predictions.

Would Andy be able to speak? Would he be able to read? If Neanderthals had such big brains, why are they generally regarded as stupid? Were they violent? Would he be a danger to the family? Would he be able to handle the frustrations, not to mention the hazards, of modern life?

Louis and I could only offer them the research notes that we had. Yes, all evidence shows that

Neanderthals did have language, although the position of the hyoid bone indicates that their voices may have been high-pitched and squeaky, and Andy might have difficulty pronouncing some of our sounds. Neanderthals also had some level of music and art. Since history is written by the victors, the assumption had always been that Neanderthals were inferior to *Homo sapiens*, but that presumption is flawed. More likely, *Homo sapiens* dominated by forming larger communities, which allowed them to combine their efforts for inventions, and, perhaps more importantly, for warfare.

"So that's why the Neanderthals were wiped out?" asked Arnie.

"Actually, they weren't wiped out," explained Louis. "Sequencing of the human genome shows that most people of European and Asian descent have some Neanderthal genes in them. *Homo sapiens* didn't eliminate the Neanderthal species. We just flooded the gene pool."

"True," I added. "About 1 to 4% of the genome of non-African modern humans comes from Neanderthals."

Arnie laughed a bit, the first sign of humor in this otherwise intense discussion. "Maybe Andy is related to us after all."

"What about his intelligence?" asked Alicia, still not ready to take the subject too lightly.

"They had large brains," I answered, "but the portion of their brain dedicated to our type of academic learning probably wasn't what took up most of the space. We know that they managed to survive under some pretty inhospitable conditions, including extremely cold weather."

"Then he should do fine here in Michigan," quipped Arnie. "We definitely have winter."

"Do you think he'd be able to read?" asked Alicia.

"Again, we don't know," replied Louis. "They seem to have been pretty good at identifying shapes and symbols, and their eyesight was probably actually a little better than ours, but, again, that part of the brain may not have been as developed as ours."

"I wouldn't count on him reading the complete works of Shakespeare," I joked. "And I doubt that he'd be the next mathematical genius, either. But my guess, and this is only a guess, is that he'd be able to read words and perform addition and subtraction."

"Drive a car?" asked Arnie.

"Maybe. Actually, I can't think of any reason why not," I answered.

"You're getting a little ahead of yourself, Larry," interjected Louis. "We don't know any of that. I'm sorry, but so much of this is guesswork."

"True," I said, "but we do know that they were problem solvers in their own habitat. The ones who lived near the sea figured out how to harvest crabs, fish, and sea birds. Those who lived inland hunted deer, mammoths, bison, and woolly rhino. They built tools with handles, and carved lightweight spears that could be thrown from up to 20 yards away with an impact sufficient for a kill. These people were innovative. They even discovered that they could access salicylic acid, which is aspirin, by chewing on poplar leaves"

"Most of the recent evidence tends to narrow the gap between their intelligence and ours," added Louis.

"What about violence?" asked Alicia. "I don't want to bring him into this world if he's going to create a danger to our family or the public."

Louis and I looked at each other, and I said, "I'll take this one.

"There's no sure way to predict who's going to become violent and who isn't. All we can tell you is that there's no evidence that Neanderthals as a group were more violent than modern humans."

"That's not saying much," groaned Arnie.

"Exactly," I added. "Modern humans probably dominated because they were the more aggressive species and were more organized in warfare. Neanderthals apparently tended to use their skills more for hunting than for combat. And we do know that they took care of each other, perhaps to a greater extent than *Homo sapiens* of that time. We've seen evidence of broken bones that had healed, indicating that group members provided for each other long enough for healing to take place. We've even heard of cases where Neanderthals survived long-term problems such as missing limbs or blindness, indicating that they took care of each other even when recovery was not to be expected."

"However, Neanderthals were pretty strong guys, so that has to be taken into consideration if you decide to raise a Neanderthal child," cautioned Louis. "Glacier Pete was only about 5'6" tall, with comparatively short arms and legs, but, like most Neanderthals, he was very muscular and had a big barrel chest. If Andy did get angry, he might hurt someone, so he'd require supervision until he learns about rules and consequences."

"That's the case with any big kid," pointed out Arnie, who routinely dealt with kids of all sizes in his physical education classes. "Will he grow faster than the other kids?"

"Maybe," I said. "Scientists can't seem to agree on that. But I'd say there's a good chance he will reach maturity a bit sooner than his classmates."

"Classmates?" said Alicia. "So, you think he could go to school."

"Unless he develops in some way that we hadn't predicted, I'd say yes," I answered. "He may not be college material, and his later years of high school might be something vocational, but still, yes."

"Would you be here to help us?" asked Arnie.

I took a deep breath. "Currently, no. I've been expelled, and Louis's application for doctoral studies has been denied.  But all that we have to offer is background information on Neanderthals.  The university has an abundant supply of professionals and programs for young children.  If you negotiate for their help, they have a lot to offer.  The administration may not appreciate the expense, but, to be honest, the heads of those departments would probably welcome the opportunity to work with this child."

"It sounds as if he might not be as different as we would have assumed," said Arnie.

"Oh, he'd definitely *look* different, and that would be a social hurdle to overcome," reminded Louis.  "Growing up is a struggle for any kid, and even more so for a kid who's different.  This kid would be different, right down to his species.  Nobody is asking you to take that lightly.

In the end, it's your call."

# CHAPTER 11: THE GRANDPARENTS

Arnie and Alicia Neill sent us back to our campsite with instructions to stay in town for a few more days. They even gave us some money for meals, along with certificates for free pizzas. I guess they remembered their own university days well enough to know that college students can survive indefinitely on pizzas. And maybe tacos, too, although we didn't have coupons for those. It was two days before we heard from the Neills again, and when we did, they told us everything that had happened in the meantime.

The morning after that late-evening visit, Alicia and Arnie dropped off Aiden at her parents' house while they spoke with their attorney. When they returned to pick him up, Aiden was napping, so Alicia and Arnie took that opportunity to sit down with her parents and explain what had happened.

Alicia's parents, Jim and Janet Andrews, were the owners of the Canadian cottages where the Neills had vacationed. Jim, a retired auto worker with a round face and a hearty laugh, was an avid hunter and fisherman who enjoyed an occasional cigar and a few more beers than his doctor would have recommended. Janet, a retired nurse, stayed mostly focused on her grown kids, her grandkids, and trying to keep up with the constant packing and unpacking for the cottage trips.

When they heard the news about Andy, there was, as expected, a moment of stunned silence. The unexpected part came when Jim's uproarious laughter suddenly penetrated the silence. "So, my second grandson is a Neanderthal? My first grandson wants to be a fairy princess for Halloween, and now you're telling me the second one is going to be a Neanderthal? What a helluva linebacker he's gonna be!" and more laughter ensued.

Janet swatted Jim's shoulder, but the tension had been broken, and real conversation began to flow.

"Yes, I've thought about that, too," said Arnie, the high school's assistant athletic director. "I'm not sure about football, because he'll be a bit on the short side, but he'll certainly have the muscles for it. I'm not sure he'll be allowed to compete, either, since he's not quite the same species as his competitors. It'll be one more controversy that we'll have to deal with."

"You'll work it out," said Jim. "I'm sure of that. If that kid was meant to come into the world, he couldn't have chosen better parents."

"I have to agree with that," said Janet with a smile.

Alicia was still processing the fact that Arnie and her dad were talking about Andy as if he was already here; as if his presence in the family was already established. It felt strange, wonderful, and more than a little empowering.

# CHAPTER 12: THE DEAL

Alicia and Arnie took some of that confidence with them to the next day's meeting with the university administration. As expected, there were intimidating faces on the other side of the table, but this time, Alicia was prepared. She had Arnie beside her, and they were accompanied by their attorney, a feisty fellow named Mr. Borgman.

After Alicia explained that she had decided against terminating the pregnancy, a Big Intimidating Guy (I'll shorten that to BIG) from the other side of the table replied, "We regret that you have chosen to ignore our best professional recommendation. You understand, of course, that if you choose to proceed with this pregnancy, it will be entirely your decision and the university will not be responsible for the outcome."

After about three seconds of silence, Mr. Borgman blurted out a loud, sarcastic laugh. "Nice try," he said to BIG. "You can drop the act now. You people know as well as we do why we are here. My client has done nothing wrong. She placed her trust in the university, and it failed her. What we are looking at here is a lawsuit that you knew full well was coming, and today's meeting is a discussion on whether an out-of-court agreement can be reached."

"It was entirely the fault of that Tanner kid," grumbled BIG. "Maybe both of them."

"Some of it was Larry's fault," said Mr. Borgman, "but even to the extent that it WAS his fault, it's still the responsibility of the university, and there were a lot of other factors that contributed to the situation. Besides, I'm sure you understand that even if it was a complete accident, even if a tree had fallen on Mrs. Neill, we would still be here. So, again, the blame-throwing is only a distraction. We are here to discuss a settlement."

Mr. Borgman opened his briefcase, pulled out several copies of the paperwork he had prepared for the meeting, and slid the copies across the table to BIG and his cronies.

"First," said Mr. Borgman, "the Neill family will require assistance from various departments throughout the university. Education, child development, occupational therapy, and psychology departments will be involved, as well as any other resources that the family deems necessary."

BIG started to open his mouth, but another administrator touched his arm to stop him.

"Second," continued Mr. Borgman, "the Neill family will require appropriate housing. They had been planning to sell their home and buy a larger one upon the arrival of their second child, but, for this child, not every house will suffice. They will need to be on or very near campus, and they will need security to protect them from aggressive media types and any other crazies who may try to harass them."

Again, BIG started to object, but this time he was interrupted by the Dean of Student Affairs. (If you recall, that's the guy who wasn't too thrilled to hear about my mistake because he was busy moving his family to a different house.) "I might be able to suggest a solution to that problem," he said.

At this point, the dean leaned forward and spoke directly to Mr. Borgman and the Neills. "As you may or may not be aware," he said, "the university recently constructed a new residence for the university president. That means that the vice president moves into the president's old house, the assistant VP moves into the VP's old house, and so on.

"I'm at the bottom of that chain. I've just finished moving my family out of the old DSA house. It's a nice two-story Victorian at the end of Oakvale Street, right next to the campus." He looked directly at Mrs. Neill as she tried to recall the house. "Back in the 60s and 70s, there was some concern that the DSA might be in danger due to student rioters, so the house was surrounded by an 8-foot-tall cement-block wall, which is now covered in ivy. The house is generally referred to as Ivy House."

"Oh, I know that house!" exclaimed Alicia. "I love it!"

"The university had been planning to convert it into office space, but they have other options for offices," continued the dean. "It has four bedrooms, big windows, 9-foot ceilings, and a huge back yard, all surrounded by that ivy-covered wall. I think it would be nearly ideal for raising a high-profile special-needs child. The house needs some upgrades in the heating and cooling system, but the university would have had to do that anyway. I believe it might be a solution to your problem."

BIG gave the dean a grumpy look, as if to say, "Whose side are you on, anyway?" and then cleared his throat and said, "Well, yes, I suppose the Neill family could rent that house for a couple of years."

Again, Mr. Borgman laughed. "You seem to have memory problems," he said to BIG. "The Neill family is not going to RENT that house, and it's not going be for just a couple of years."

"Well, I'm not going to just GIVE them the house!" bellowed BIG.

"Actually, you probably would, if we insisted on it," replied Mr. Borgman, "because it would be a lot cheaper than the multi-million-dollar settlement that the university would be paying out if we took this to court. But the Neills aren't asking for that. They will sell their current home, which is smaller but newer than the Ivy House, and the university will accept that as full payment for the Ivy House. The Neill family will own the house, and the only stipulation is that whenever, and if ever, they decide to sell it, the university will have the option to buy it back at 80% of its market value."

BIG grumbled but did not object. The group went on to examine the rest of Alicia and Arnie's demands. The next one read: "The Neanderthal specialists, Louis and Lawrence Tanner, will be returned to their positions at the university, where they will continue their studies and serve as advisors to the Neill family."

BIG started bellowing again. Apparently bellowing came naturally to him, and Alicia could almost envision him as a toddler throwing a temper tantrum in his high chair. To be fair, it was the university's budget and reputation (as well as his own reputation) that he was trying to protect, and, to be fair again, he had every right to be furious at me. Bellowing was all he had to work with at this time, and he knew it, so he was determined to use it for all it was worth.

"Those idiots created this problem, and I have no intention of ever allowing either of them on this campus again!" he (you guessed it) bellowed.

"Those 'idiots' are this university's best authorities on Neanderthals," Borgman reminded him, "and they have spent months examining the cell structures of the glacier man from whom this child was cloned. Furthermore, Mr. and Mrs. Neill have consulted with the brothers and are comfortable with their input. Having them on scene is a non-negotiable necessity."

Alicia told me later that BIG's face turned beet red and he looked as if he was going to blow a gasket.

Thinking of my dad, back when his car got impounded, I could almost feel sorry for the guy. Almost.

"These are enormous expenses for the university," complained BIG.

"Actually, they aren't," said Borgman, "and you know it. Besides, the university will find ways to use all of this publicity to its advantage. Pine State is going to be just fine."

Borgman picked up his briefcase, escorted Alicia and Arnie out of the building, and told the university reps to get back with him when they had reached their conclusion.

The next day, he received a message from the university's legal staff that all conditions would be met. The university's only request was that the agreement would remain private until the Neanderthal child was born, and that in the event that he did not survive the pregnancy, the university would keep Ivy House.

Alicia and Arnie had no problem with that. The papers were signed the next day.

~~~

A week later, September 11, 2001, the world watched in horror as planes crashed into the twin towers of the World Trade Center, the Pentagon, and a field in Pennsylvania. Alicia told me that she couldn't help wondering whether Andy would be any better off in this world than in the one that would have greeted him 40,000 years ago, but there was no looking back now. All systems were go.

# CHAPTER 13: THE ARRIVAL

Louis and I moved into an apartment above the garage at one of the other Victorian houses just down the block from Ivy House. Our first step was to get caught up on our classes, since we had started the term a few days late. Every other spare minute was spent preparing for Andy's arrival and the media blitz that would follow.

For the moment, everything was a tightly-protected secret. Alicia's friends and co-workers knew she was pregnant, but aside from her parents, and Arnie's parents who lived in Florida, nobody knew anything about the strange circumstances of the pregnancy.

I accompanied Alicia to some of her appointments at the clinic to advise her doctors, as well as I could, about what to expect from a Neanderthal pregnancy. However, it had been decided that she would not be giving birth at our local hospital. Dr. Tremblay had recommended a hospital in southern Ontario where he had previously worked. He said he had great faith in that hospital and it would be easier to shield Alicia and Andy from the press at that location. Being born in Canada would also give Andy dual Canadian/American citizenship, which might come in handy in the future. Alicia agreed. Besides, she and her brother and her father co-owned the three Canadian cottages, so it did seem to make sense.

At Christmas, Louis and I spent only three days visiting our parents, and the rest of the ten-day break helping the Neills move into Ivy House. Aiden, now almost three years old, ran gleefully through the house. He was particularly fascinated by the fact that the kitchen was accessible from either the dining room or the hall, meaning that he could run in a full circle through the main floor of the house, with Gus, the dog, following close behind. Aiden loved the back yard, too, because one side of it had a downward slope, so Louis and I took turns pushing him on his sled and helping him pull it back up to the house. When we weren't moving furniture or keeping Aiden and Gus occupied, Louis and I painted walls, unpacked boxes, and washed windows. I'm not sure how Louis felt about it, but, for me, it was a welcome opportunity to accomplish something physically useful and to escape from the stress of the events that had taken place and the ones that we knew would follow.

~~~

Andrew James Neill was born by Cesarean section at 11:53 a.m. on February 18, 2002. It had been exactly 11 months since Louis and I had discovered Glacier Pete, but somehow it felt as if decades had passed. Or maybe 40,000 years.

Andy was the cutest baby imaginable. His protruding cheekbones and slightly larger nose gave his face a pudgy appearance that made him irresistible. He already had a pretty good mop of wavy reddish hair, and it wasn't long before his wide smile appeared. When Alicia returned to Michigan and allowed me to hold him, I felt like an uncle or something, and the guilt that I had been carrying over this whole event was gone, at least for the moment. We all just basked in the miracle of this amazing new person.

Most of the staff at the maternity hospital in Ontario had known only that Mrs. Neill was having a C-section. They didn't know why, and Andy's appearance at birth would not have immediately given it away. Neanderthal adults had considerably larger skulls than modern humans, but, as an evolutionary adaptation to limit difficult births, most of that growth occurred in a growth spurt during the first few months following birth.

The few hospital staff members who did know about Andy's heritage were more than happy to keep their mouths shut until Mrs. Neill and the baby were safely at home and an official press release could be made. Ontario has reporters, too, and the staff had no desire to see them crowding into the hospital.

It was the calm before the storm.

# PART 2: AFTER

Toddler Andy

# CHAPTER 14: THE MEDIA STORM

When the press release occurred, a week after Andy's birth, Louis and I were prepared, or at least as prepared as possible under the circumstances. For months we had been working alongside the university's P.R. department, sharing our knowledge with them and contributing to decisions about how to word the announcements. We also understood that the original announcements would be only the beginning of the storm. There would be thousands of questions to be answered, some of them quite reasonable and some based on rampant paranoia. We did everything in our power to be ready, but we also knew that it would never be enough.

The campus security guards and local police were ready, too. Security around the university was increased, but especially around the neighborhood where the Neills lived. That also happened to be the neighborhood where Louis and I lived, which was convenient for us because I'm pretty sure the administration wasn't remotely concerned about our well-being. Nevertheless, they seemed to have reluctantly accepted that we could contribute something, even if it was only damage-control for damage that we had created.

Before the press release even occurred, the university P.R. department provided Louis and me with a schedule of interviews. We would appear alongside doctors and administrators on local newscasts and national broadcasts, and appear again, more as targets than guests, on in-depth investigative programs. We also provided information to national and international newspapers and magazines.

Louis was comfortable with writing articles for Time Magazine and Scientific American, but less comfortable with appearing on 60-Minutes. I took the central speaking role when I could, but Louis knew he couldn't completely avoid it this time. Alicia and Arnie couldn't completely avoid the publicity either, but their exposure was kept to a minimum. The university stuck to releasing only still photos or 30-second videos of the parents with their new baby. For his own safety, Aiden was kept completely out of the picture.

I didn't mind providing facts to honest journalists. It was the tabloid stuff that drove me crazy. Tabloid journalists don't want facts. They only want to introduce scary or disturbing questions. In this case, it was stuff like, "Will the Pine State Cave Man be a Danger to Humanity?" or "Are Neanderthals Getting a Second Chance to Destroy Us?" Of course, I volunteered to submit articles or appear on their broadcasts, but they rarely accepted. The truth would have been far less sensational than the scary nonsense they had fabricated. All we could do was keep trying and keep waiting until some other hot news story blew us off of the front pages.

Meanwhile, the university's tech department did what it could to keep the public informed about the *real* life of Andy and his family. Facebook and Instagram had not yet been created, and even MySpace was a year away, so the techies settled for setting up a page on the university's website to display pictures and updates of Andy and his family. It got thousands of visitors.

As we expected, the publicity mess would never go away completely. It would raise its ugly head again when Andy attended grade school. It would pop up every time he did or said anything controversial. And whenever it did, we would be there. For better or worse, Louis and I were permanently bonded to Andy and his family.

# CHAPTER 15: THE FIRST YEAR

Someday, a decade or so in the future, Andy would struggle with the fact that he had been launched thousands of years into the future, created in a laboratory, and born to a mother of a slightly different species.  But, as a newborn, he didn't know about any of that, and he certainly didn't care.  He had nine months to bond with Alicia in her womb, and when he emerged into daylight, he seemed delighted to meet her.  His tiny hands tried to grasp her blond hair as his big blue eyes attempted to focus on her face.  He was a happy baby.

He was also a hungry baby.  Neanderthal babies have a growth spurt in the early months, especially in the skull bones, requiring enormous amounts of nutrition.  In their native times, that may have contributed to high infant mortality rates because only well-nourished mothers could support that demand.  Alicia nursed him almost constantly, supplementing once daily with a special high-protein, high-calcium, vitamin-enriched formula that had been developed by his pediatricians.  Apparently, it worked, because he grew and developed perfectly, or at least as perfectly as we could guess from our research on Neanderthal bone specimens.  Today's world also protected him from lead exposure, which was another hazard of babies during his ancestors' time.

But Andy wasn't always free to rest in his mother's arms and reach for her hair.  Even more than his *Homo sapiens* infant counterparts, he was constantly being removed for some sort of medical analysis or evaluation.  He was the constant subject of blood tests, ultrasounds, and CT scans.  It seemed that every second or third day, he was looking up at masked medical professionals doing something or other to him.  His doctors had determined that his greatest impairment in modern society might be an inability to pronounce modern vowel sounds, so, less than a month after his birth, he underwent his first surgery on his hyoid bone and larynx.  He came home so traumatized that Alicia declared "never again."  He got over it, though, and eventually she agreed to a second surgery at age three.  The third surgery, if it happened, would occur at puberty, and by then Andy himself would be in a position to make the decision.

The doctors' other great concern was immunity or lack thereof.  Anyone who has studied Native American history knows that even when the indigenous people weren't being intentionally targeted for genocide, whole villages were wiped out by foreign viruses such as influenza.  Andy's doctors were doing everything in their power to avoid anything like that.  Breastfeeding might help, as it would pass along some of Alicia's immunity, but it might not be enough.  He got all of his vaccinations on schedule, but he wouldn't be eligible for the flu shot until age 6 months, so it was important to protect him until that time.

Alicia had left her teaching job at the end the fall semester before Andy was born. Not only did she need time to care for a three-year-old and a unique newborn, she was concerned that working in a crowded school might expose her to viruses that could be deadly to Andy. And, although she hadn't told the school administrators at the time of her resignation, she also knew that her presence at the school would place them in the middle of a media firestorm, which they undoubtedly would prefer to avoid.

Not that they could avoid it entirely. Arnie did not resign. He settled for reminding his students that his athletic program had zero-tolerance for harassment of anyone including himself. Students who were caught snickering or making cave-man comments found themselves facing detention. He did, however, grant an interview with a student reporter from the school newspaper, including a picture of himself with his new baby (taken before Andy's head-growth spurt) and his concerns for the health of his newborn son. Then he returned to his usual routine of pursuing excellence in the school's sports programs, leaving the students little time or energy for snarky remarks.

Nor could Alicia completely avoid controversy by staying at home. Protestors from all sides of the political spectrum elevated her to some sort of extreme status. Anti-abortion groups wanted to claim her as their current hero for choosing to give birth to Andy. She replied by saying that under slightly different circumstances, she might have made a different choice, and she was grateful that the decision had been hers to make. An opposing group insisted that she should never have been allowed to bring a "prehistoric monster" into the world. A third group insisted that she was an unwilling participant in a government plot to eliminate modern humans and replace us with a more gullible, compliant species.

Whenever Alicia informed me of groups like the latter two, I did everything in my power to reach them and provide a more realistic viewpoint. I told the "prehistoric monster" group that Andy would be subject to the same laws as everyone else, and that if he got into any legal trouble, he would be jailed just like the rest of us. I had to fend off ridiculous assumptions that he would be able to break out of jail, or that he would be eating the neighbor's cats and dogs. Very few of these group members appeared to believe me, but I hoped I had planted seeds of reason that might grow in at least a few of them.

The "government conspiracy" groups were harder to reason with because they assumed that I was part of the conspiracy, so I focused on the reproductive angle: "Let's do the math," I said. "It's all fractions. Andy is only one person. If he reproduces, it will be with a *Homo sapiens* female. The offspring would be only half Neanderthal, and, since they wouldn't be allowed to mate with each other, the next generation would be only a quarter Neanderthal, and so on, until the Neanderthal genes became what they already are: a small portion of our *Homo sapiens* genome." I handed out flyers and made Power Point presentations. Some people nodded, but the overall impact on the crowd was not what I had hoped. I'd always been the guy who could work a crowd. What did I need to do differently?

Somewhere along the line, I realized that what was missing from my presentation was humor. These people wanted stress-relief, and I could provide that if I set my mind to it. The next time, I was ready with a different type of photos loaded onto my power point presentation:

"This, my friends, is our prehistoric monster," I began, displaying a close-up picture of baby Andy's chubby face with a pouty or grumpy expression. (I got my best shots when he was pooping.) "This one is even more frightening," I would add, showing another ridiculous grumpy-baby picture, and another one after that. By that time, the audience was laughing, so I would continue, "But it's not his face that's so frightening, it's his superior strength," while displaying a two-second clip of Andy dropping his bottle on his foot.

After that humor had been established, I would say, "Okay, it's time to get serious now. Here's a picture of Glacier Pete from whom Andy was cloned." Having seen Alicia's response to the actual photo of Glacier

Pete, I substituted an artist's rendition, drawn to scale but with a much livelier smiling face, and one arm raised in a waving motion. "He was 5'6" tall. That's pretty scary," I said with an eye-roll. More laughter. "But it's really about those muscles. He definitely has bigger calves and arms than I do. If Glacier Pete had challenged me to an arm-wrestling match, you'd be wise to bet your money on him, because he'd have my wimpy arm flat on the table before I could say ouch!" Grins from the audience. "But could he win against one of our NFL linebackers or one of our Olympic weightlifters or heavyweight boxers? Maybe not, because here's the thing: Glacier Pete was just a guy, not Superman. He couldn't leap tall buildings in a single bound. He couldn't bend steel bars with his bare hands. He was just a guy.

"We have no reason to believe that Glacier Pete was violent. He didn't die in combat," I continued, this time in a much more somber tone. "It appears that he got caught in a blizzard while hunting for food, and he froze to death. In fact, our evidence shows that Neanderthals tended to avoid combat as much as possible. They were probably driven out by people whose advantage was larger armies.

"The events of 9/11 are still fresh in our minds. Did those terrorists have big muscles? I don't know. Did they? What they had were big airplanes. In our society, the danger is not from the guys with the biggest biceps. It's from the guys who can buy, steal, or, in this case, hijack the biggest weapons."

I flipped to another picture of baby Andy, this time smiling and propped up against Gus. "Ladies and Gentlemen, this is not our enemy. Thank you for your time, and please be safe."

This presentation was a hit! I posted it on websites and sent it through mass emails. I even gave a variation of it on talk shows. It seemed to have the desired effect. The United States had enemies at that time, and sometimes it was hard to tell exactly who they were. But Andy, at least for the moment, was not on the list.

As spring rolled into summer, life became a bit more normal at Ivy House. I saw Andy a couple of times a week, and his specialists continued to visit occasionally, but Louis and I were busy with summer classes, and the Neills had more time to just be a family. They were even given permission to leave for six weeks in the summer for their annual vacation to Canada. To protect their privacy, the university lent them one of its leased vans so that their vehicle would not be tracked to the vacation spot. They needed some peace and quiet for a while, and so did I. Louis and I visited our parents for a couple of weeks and even got in some beach time. I brought my guitar with me for evenings at the fireside, and hoped that the Neills were doing the same.

~~~

Usually, my visits to the Neill home took place during the daytime hours, but one day that autumn I stopped by to pick up some paperwork that I had forgotten, and I happened to arrive just after Aiden and Andy had been put to bed. Aiden had gone to sleep immediately, but Andy wasn't remotely interested in sleeping. He had reached the stage where babies crawl, but, for Andy, that also meant a lot of climbing. Trying to keep him in bed was a near impossibility.

Arnie and Alicia sat sprawled on the sofa, looking exhausted as thumping noises emanated from Andy's bedroom. "It's your turn," said Alicia in a weary tone. Arnie groaned, gave me a weak grin, and said, "You've gotta see this," as he walked to Andy's bedroom. I followed and watched from outside the bedroom door.

Andy's room had 9-foot ceilings with carved crown moldings and an antique light fixture hanging from the center. A row of large, multi-pane windows lined the wall across from the entrance, and in the corner to my left, Gus slept, or attempted to sleep, on his cushioned dog bed. Andy's crib stood in the center, with the head end up against the windows. A chair stood next to it where his mother sat when she read stories to him. Inside the crib were several stuffed toys, including a woolly mammoth from the movie *Ice Age*. But Andy himself was not in the crib. Dressed in his footed fleece pajamas, he was literally climbing the curtains and had made it about halfway up to the curtain rod. Arnie plucked him from the curtain, moved the crib a bit farther from the windows, put him back to bed, and returned to the living room.

A couple of thumps later, Arnie looked at Alicia and said, "Your turn." I followed Alicia, and this time Andy was climbing over the side rail. When she put him back into bed and raised the rails as high as they would go, Andy took one of his toys and tossed it across the room, narrowly missing Gus, who scampered out of his bed. Alicia dragged Gus's dog crate into the room, propped the crate door open, and moved his dog bed inside so Gus would be protected from flying objects. Then she left the room.

The next sound we heard wasn't a thump, it was more of a creaking sound. "Your turn again," said Alicia. When I followed Arnie into the room, Andy had climbed to a precarious spot on the foot end of the crib and was reaching for the hanging light fixture. Arnie plucked him off of his perch and set him on the floor while Arnie moved the crib again.

But this time, Andy was fascinated by Gus's crate. Deciding that Gus's toys were more interesting than his own, Andy crawled into the crate, picked up one of Gus's big rubber toys, gnawed on the dog toy for a few seconds, and curled up contentedly in the back of the crate. Gus trotted out of the crate and jumped up on the reading chair.

Arnie examined the situation for a moment, decided it worked, and closed the door of the dog crate.

As we stepped out of the room, I saw Gus jump into the empty crib and curl up next to the stuffed woolly mammoth.

Arnie returned to the sofa and told Alicia, "I think we can go to bed now," adding, "Don't ask."

"Okay, I won't," she answered.

As I left the house, I knew that Alicia's parents were right: these two were the perfect parents for Andy.

# CHAPTER 16: THE EARLY YEARS

The next few years were busy times at the Neill home, especially during the warmer months when activities could be moved outdoors. The backyard at Ivy House had been stocked with a phenomenal assortment of outdoor play equipment, much of it donated by the manufacturers. Swings, tube-style slides, climbing ropes, a dome-shaped jungle gym, a Slip-N-Slide, and even a bounce house were installed within the ivy-covered walls for the Neill boys and their visitors. Students from the Early Childhood Development (ECD) program at the college took turns spending time at the house, showering attention on both Andy and Aiden. Andy, of course, was their primary interest, but they understood family dynamics enough to know that Aiden could become the family's "lost child" if he spent his entire youth in the shadow of his famous younger brother. Besides, Andy adored Aiden, so it was easy to include both of them even though Aiden was three years older.

Other parents in the neighborhood, most of whom were staff members at the university, had gotten to know Alicia and Arnie, and had been assured by the ECD staff that it was safe for their children to play with Andy and Aiden at Ivy House. Since I was usually the only adult male on site (Arnie was at work) I was often the rough-and-tumble guy, catching a Nerf football that had been thrown an impressive three feet, and then carefully and dramatically falling to the ground as eight giggling preschoolers tackled me.

Nearly all of these activities were supervised by student aides who took notes on Andy's physical and social development. The backyard environment was carefully controlled.

There were, however, occasional "security issues" to be dealt with; nothing dangerous, just nuisance stuff. I was standing in the back yard with Arnie one day just before the children arrived, when a buzzing noise alerted us to a camera drone overhead. Arnie scowled and mumbled something about target practice as he stepped inside for a moment and grabbed something from an overhead cabinet. With his hand behind his back and some paper towels sticking out of his pockets, he stepped quietly back outside, staying close to the ivy-covered walls. Was that a gun behind his back? I had never known Arnie to have weapons in the house, but this wasn't the time to ask, so I just watched. After a moment, Arnie took aim and fired. The camera drone disappeared for an instant into a splash of yellow paint and then flopped to the ground, where Arnie stomped on it and dropped it into the trash before cleaning up the yellow paint with his paper towels. "I used to be on the paintball team," he grinned.

~~~

Of course, I, and occasionally Louis, also took notes comparing Andy's structure and function with the information on Neanderthals that we had gathered before he came into the picture. For us, though, Andy was much more than a statistic. He and his family had become our family.

Fortunately, we didn't need to override any of those family prejudices in order to make an honest assessment of Andy during those toddler years. He was just a normal kid. He wasn't a perfect kid – he did occasionally let out a shriek of frustration or take a swat at someone who interfered with his activities – but it was nothing remotely out of the ordinary for a child of his age, according to the ECD students and staff.

He was however, slightly larger and much stronger than others kids his age, which created a bit of confusion and a fair level of danger to himself. His climbing was exceptional, which brings us to the subject of headgear.

Within a day or two after Andy was born, he had been fitted with a soft foam helmet designed to guide his skull growth in a slightly more modern-human direction. His parents were advised to remove the helmet if it seemed to be causing him discomfort, but they left it on as much as possible to protect him from his self-inflicted injuries. Because of his rapid growth, he was provided with a larger helmet each week, and he had been wearing one on the night when I watched him climbing out of his crib. By the time he reached his toddler years, he was only expected to wear the helmet when he slept, but Alicia was a bit reluctant to take it off of him at playtime. His strength often carried him to the top of the jungle gym or even to the top of the swing set, which wasn't designed to be climbed. But his coordination still wasn't the greatest, so it wasn't unusual for him to fall. Alicia or the students tried to be available to watch him at all times, but that's always an imperfect process, so Alicia preferred to keep the helmet on. When Andy started noticing that the other kids weren't wearing helmets, their mothers responded by sending them to Ivy House wearing their bike helmets, which offered those parents a bit of security regarding their own kids' skulls while easing Alicia's mind a bit.

So, Andy continued to climb and tumble and swing and push and run in the big back yard at Ivy House. His physical achievements were more on a level with Aiden and his friends, although they understood that Andy was one of "the little kids" in terms of his ability to speak and to understand complex games.

But the good news was that although Andy's intellectual abilities weren't as advanced as his physical abilities, they were still pretty much on target for his age category. He understood words and concepts as well as any toddler, although pronouncing words was still a struggle for him. When he turned three, Alicia reluctantly consented to that second laryngeal surgery.

This time, though, Andy took it pretty much in stride. He ate lots of ice cream and pudding for the next couple of weeks, and he only missed a few days of his climbing.

Andy was a determined little boy, and nothing was going to slow him down.

# CHAPTER 17: GRADE SCHOOL

It's common for parents to get a little emotional when their child starts kindergarten, and for Alicia that emotion was compounded by the risks. Andy would no longer be protected by his foam helmet or the brick walls at Ivy House. Security at the school was beefed up on the day that he arrived, but Alicia still worried a bit about the crazy people who might think Andy was some creature to be feared. As always, the tabloid press fed those fears with headlines like, "Neanderthal in School: Is He a Miracle or a Menace?" and "Parents Rush to Remove Children from Neanderthal Classroom." In reality, exactly eight children had withdrawn from that entire elementary school that year, and in every case it was because their parents, who had been grad students or adjunct professors at the college, had moved on to other jobs.

I continued to fend off the press as much as possible, and I stayed close to Andy and his family, sharing in the challenges that they faced throughout his school years.

And Andy, at 5 ½ years old, was ready and eager to start kindergarten. He had attended a small preschool the year before, and Alicia had returned to her job as a high school English teacher. Andy greeted his new classmates with his wide grin and strong hugs and enjoyed being the teacher's helper when chairs and tables needed to be moved. Academically, he learned his letters and numbers at about the same rate as his classmates. His teacher encouraged each child to develop individually, and that included Andy. On the rare occasion that Andy did or said something wrong, all she had to do was remind him to be kind, and he quickly said he was sorry. The year flew by.

First and second grades were a different story. Teachers, as a whole, are amazing, but there are always a few who are too exhausted, overwhelmed, or stressed out to care. So, in grades 1 and 2, Andy had teachers who already had too many students in their classes and just wished they didn't have to deal with this one. To make it worse, the students were learning to read, and Andy was struggling with that. His physical development had reached the point where his large head began to look distinctly different from his classmates', and because his adult teeth had emerged a full two years before the *Homo sapiens* kids', he was already wearing braces. Combine all of that, and he became a target for bullies.

One Autumn day when Andy was crossing the schoolyard behind the gym, he was shoved to the ground from behind. Picking himself up from the dirt, he found himself facing a smirking fellow 2nd grader and two of the kid's buddies. "What's the matter, Cave Man? That big brain of yours can't figure out how to read?" sneered the bully. Before Andy could answer, he was looking at the back of the blue shirt that he had seen Aiden wearing that morning. In 5th grade, and tall by nature, Aiden was nearly a foot taller than the bully.

"Is there a problem here?" asked Aiden in the deepest voice he could manage. The bully grumbled and walked away, followed by his friends. Turning to Andy, Aiden said, "Let me know if anything like that happens again. Or let a teacher know. Nobody has the right to treat you that way." Then Aiden returned to his 5th grade classmates.

Actually, Aiden had relished his first three years at school without Andy. Aiden was academically brilliant and was just relieved to be in a place where he could be himself instead of watching all of the attention focused on his controversial little brother. But this was the first time Aiden had realized how damaging that attention could be for Andy. When Aiden talked it over with his mother that evening, she sighed and nodded and showed Aiden the newspaper headlines from Andy's first day at school. "He will get a lot of attention throughout his life," she told Aiden, "and most of it will be the kind he'll wish he could avoid. Thank you for helping him, but don't endanger yourself. Get adults to help you if you see this sort of thing again."

After that incident, the school kept a closer eye on its potential bullies, but Andy still struggled with reading. He seemed to have the capability but not the patience. "I hate reading," Andy told his father. "And I hate Clifford," referring to the *Clifford the Big Red Dog* books that the children were assigned to read.

"Do you like cars and tractors?" asked Arnie.

"Yeah!" replied Andy.

"Would you like to drive them someday, and maybe work on them?"

"Yeah!"

"Great!" said Arnie, "but in order to do that, you're going to have to learn to read, at least a little bit. People who drive cars have to be able to read the signs that say 'stop' and 'no left turn' and 'next exit.' I'll work with you on it. You can sit on my lap and we'll read the Sunday comics together. We'll take it a word or two at a time. We'll get there," he said, and hugged his little boy.

Over the summer months, Arnie kept his promise. Alicia and Arnie discovered the *Magic Tree House Facts* books, which covered dinosaurs, mummies and pyramids, knights and castles, narwhals and whales, and other wonderful things.

When Andy started third grade, he was surprised to see four other boys lined up enthusiastically in front of the new teacher's desk. These were the boys who disliked the second grade books just as much as Andy did, so he hadn't expected to hear them telling her, "You just have to get the *I Survived* books! You have to get them!" Andy had never heard of the books, and, until then, neither had Alicia. As it turned out, they are books that tell a historical story through the eyes of a fictional kid who lived to tell the tale. At that time, *I Survived the Shark Attacks of 1916* had just come out, following *I Survived the Sinking of the Titanic, 1912* from two months earlier. Later that school year it was followed by *I Survived Hurricane Katrina, 2005.* These books helped Andy and his fellow slow readers discover a real excitement for reading.

It had taken him a little while to get there, and Andy might still never be the guy who reads the complete works of Shakespeare, but he was done being the kid who had a big brain but couldn't read.

Better yet, he knew that when he got old enough, the Neanderthal kid who had been mocked and shoved would someday cruise by in an automobile, or operate an excavator at a construction site, or maybe even fly a plane. The possibilities were endless, and he would explore them all.

# CHAPTER 18: THE MIDDLE YEARS

Ten-year-old Andy scowled at the food on his plate. "I hate mixed vegetables," he grumbled, adding proudly, "I'm Neanderthal! Neanderthals didn't eat mixed vegetables. They ate mammoths! And bison! And woolly rhinos!" He gestured dramatically.

"They also didn't eat pizza or tacos or ice cream with pineapple topping," deadpanned Alicia without looking up from her work in the kitchen. "Eat your vegetables."

"Vegetables are what food eats," grumbled Andy.

~~~

It was one of many stories that Alicia shared with me as Andy reached Grade 5. I observed him coming into his own as a distinct personality and also as a typical 10-year-old. His parents had enrolled him in Cub Scouts back in the first grade, so this was the year he would advance to Boy Scouts. The crafts and camping suited him and served as a welcome relief from the classroom.

He was also learning to play the guitar, first from me, and then from a music teacher. He had tried the trumpet and the piano, but the guitar seemed to suit him better. It was something he could carry with him, and the music could be anything from soft and soothing to an unplugged version of heavy metal, depending on the circumstances.

Like the guitar, Andy had become, if nothing else, adaptable. He was the resilient kid who could take almost anything in stride and keep moving forward no matter what happened. His mother called him "a determined little boy," and he definitely was. If he wanted to achieve something, nothing could stop him. He viewed it as part of his Neanderthal heritage, and maybe it was, but whatever it was, it was serving him well in the 21st Century.

Andy's physical development was making the process easier as he got older, although that brought its own challenges. He matured slightly faster than his classmates, so although he wasn't much taller than they were, he was considerably and obviously more muscular. It meant that most of the other boys didn't try to bully him, but there's always an exception to the rule, especially when the bully is older.

When Andy was in the 6th grade, a taller but thinner 7th grader intentionally knocked Andy's books out of his arms. When Andy bent over to pick them up, the kid shoved Andy head first into a tree trunk. Angry and in pain, Andy charged at the kid, tackling him at the hips, lifting him into the air, and dumping the bully head first into the bushes.

By this time, the incident had drawn the attention of several other kids in the schoolyard, as well as a few staff members who escorted both boys into the principal's office. "He tried to kill me!" accused the bully, looking directly at Andy and adding, "He's a prehistoric savage who should go back to his cave!"

The bully had hoped to goad Andy into another fight, but Andy wasn't taking the bait. He just showed the principal his scraped ear and gashed forehead, and said, "That's where he rammed my head into a tree after he knocked my books out of my hands."

School security cameras and the testimony of other students confirmed Andy's story but, as expected, he wasn't off the hook. Both boys were given detention, and Andy got lectures from both the school officials and his parents about the dangers of fighting.

"You were justified in defending yourself," said Arnie, who encountered this sort of thing with his high school Phys Ed students more often than he cared to discuss, "but you dropped him on his head. What if his neck had broken? He could have died or become paralyzed. And I guess you know that the media are going to have a field day with this."

"What was I supposed to do? Let him bash my head in?" yelled Andy, fighting back tears. "And yes, I know all about the media. They'll call me a cave man and say I'm dangerous and should be kicked out of school. So, does that mean that I have to be more perfect than everyone else just because of who I am? I'm sick of being Neanderthal! I hate school, and I hate my life!" He ran into his bedroom and slammed the door behind him.

A few minutes later, Alicia entered his room, hugged him and said, "It might seem awful right now, but this will blow over. You're a good kid, and anybody who knows you already knows that. As for the kid who shoved you, I found out this is his third offense, and Child Protective Services is looking into it. It appears that he may have an abusive alcoholic father."

"Right now, I don't care," mumbled Andy.

"Your dad will be enrolling you in an Aikido class. It will help you learn ways to defend yourself without inflicting unnecessary damage to anyone. Adults take the class, too, so they can defend themselves without danger of lawsuits," Alicia said. Then she went to the kitchen and brought him a bowl of ice cream with pineapple topping on it. It seemed to soothe the injuries to both his forehead and his mind.

Arnie had been right about the media response, but this was 2013 and a few things had changed since Andy was born and even since he started school. Social media had taken hold, and the security camera video of the fight went viral. Millions of people viewed it, and it was shown on TV celebrity reports. The video was only a grainy, black-and-white image, but it told the story. Discussion threads went wild, but the general consensus was on Andy's side. As his parents had predicted, it blew over.

None of this is meant to suggest that fighting was Andy's only physical activity. Remember, his father was, and still is, a high-school athletic director, and ever since Andy was born, Arnie had been attempting to work out Andy's place in the athletic system. During his grade school years, it hadn't been too much of an issue because there were no competitive sports. Well, none except Little League, which Arnie coached. The league wouldn't allow Andy to compete, but he showed up for practice and was an excellent hitter and base runner. His eyesight and coordination, as well as his muscles, put him in a category that even Arnie couldn't claim would be fair to the other kids his age. To Arnie's great relief, Andy didn't seem to mind limiting his participation to practice and spectating. Andy didn't much care for the public spotlight and the criticism and the pressure to win, so he was fine with the practice field and the bleachers and the hot dogs.

When he arrived in junior high, the issue of competitive sports came up again, and it was handled on a sport-by-sport basis. Andy wasn't interested in football, so that decision didn't have to be made. He was too short for basketball, so that wasn't an issue either. Mostly, he just didn't care much for team sports, so that left only individual sports to be dealt with and, of course, gym class.

Although Andy had exceptionally strong muscles, his chunky body weight made him only average at such things as rope climbing and pull-ups. He was great at running the 50-yard dash, but not so great at longer distances due to his shorter legs and, again, stocky build. He was good at gymnastics and swimming, and great at wrestling and weight lifting, but the conference wouldn't allow him to compete, which didn't bother him at all. He was offered the opportunity to do exhibition performances in gymnastics and weight lifting, but he firmly declined. The school settled for putting "Personal Best" plaques for him in the hallway, and he was okay with that. Andy's strength was his gift, and he wanted to develop it for his own satisfaction, not for competitive purposes.

~~~

Although Andy tended to avoid the spotlight, he was far from shy. He had an addictive smile and a wit that took people by surprise. His sense of humor may have been partly inherited, but it was also developed through practice and circumstances. Since he was almost constantly in a position of having to deflect wise-crack remarks, his parents and I helped him practice the art of humor. Many a nasty interaction can be prevented by appropriately placed humor, especially the self-deprecating kind. His Aikido classes were teaching him how to deflect physical attacks, and I worked with him on deflecting the verbal ones.

"Whenever possible, agree with the heckler," I advised, recalling my own experiences as a teen. "For example, when a heckler asks, 'Are you headed back to your cave now?' say something like, 'Yeah, I guess I'll eat a few rocks for dinner.'"

"Seasoned with a rat or two," chimed in Andy, catching on quickly.

Getting to the more sensitive subjects, I made another example. "Busted any heads lately?" I asked.

Andy grimaced for a moment, then smiled and offered with a grin, "Only the people who annoy me."

"Excellent!" I proclaimed. "Okay, now how about the jerks who feel the need to insult your intellect? You and I both know there's nothing wrong with your intellect, but some people will try to create that problem. So, again, meet sarcasm with sarcasm."

After a moment's thought, Andy said, "Last week I was walking into the school supply store and some kid asked me if I was planning to buy myself a brain. I couldn't think of anything to say back to him."

"What would you say if he asked you again today? Remember, agree with him if possible."

After a moment, Andy answered, "Yeah, my current brain still has some good miles left on it, but I like to keep a spare on hand for emergencies."

"Perfect!" I said. "Never be mean, and always speak with a smile, not a smirk. Learn the difference between friendly sarcasm and mean spirited snarkyness, and don't cross the line unless you have to. Got it?"

"Got it!" he answered.

I left with the strange sense of satisfaction that my own history as a Lamebrain had actually taught me something that I could share with Andy.

# CHAPTER 19: RETURNING A FAVOR

The junior high and high school buildings were back to back, so it happened on one spring day that Andy had just left his 8th grade classes at the end of the day when he saw two high school boys shoving a slim, blond-haired boy against the outside wall of the high school gym. "Bullies again," sighed Andy, wondering where these guys come from and why they don't just get a life. As he walked closer, Andy could hear insults being hurled by the two bullies, and he could finally get a good look at the bruised face of the victim. To his horror, he saw that it was Aiden.

This might be a good time to point out that although Andy was only 14, Neanderthals mature somewhat faster than *Homo sapiens*, so Andy was almost a fully grown adult. His height wasn't any greater than the boys he was approaching, but his build would have left an onlooker thinking that a short man with shoulder-length bushy red hair and large muscles was approaching three slender boys. Taking a deep breath and trying to remember everything he'd been taught, Andy sneaked up from behind and suddenly stepped between Aiden and the bullies, just as Aiden had done for him back in the second grade. His presence startled the bullies to the point where they stopped for an instant.

Andy had undergone his third throat surgery the previous summer, so his voice, though it still had a nasal tone, had lost that high pitch that annoyed him during his younger years. Today, he would make good use of his new, deeper voice. Pressing his wide grin, his protruding brow, and his enormous nose just inches from the bully's face, he said, "Do we have a problem here?"

"The problem is your pansy brother," said the bully, letting out a list of homophobic slurs that I'll choose not to repeat here. "We don't need him and his buddies around here!"

"No-o-o, I believe YOU are the one creating a problem today," said Andy calmly with a fake grin. Then, stepping back a bit closer to Aiden, he said in an artificially pleasant, matter-of-fact voice, "Leave.

Just.

Leave."

As Andy told me later, he spent a tense moment trying to remember everything he had learned in his Aikido classes and was prepared to deflect blows and slow-roll this jerk to the pavement if necessary. However, by that time Aiden had recovered from his impact with the building and was standing immediately beside Andy, taller and doing his own version of an intimidating glare. The bully picked up his backpack, growled a few more slurs, and left with his accomplice, insisting that he'd be back later.

After the bullies left, Andy led Aiden to a bench, reached into his own backpack, and handed Aiden some Kleenex and a can of soda pop he had purchased from the vending machine just before he'd arrived on this scene. "Are you okay?" Andy asked.

"I'll survive," was Aiden's frustrated reply. He held the cold beverage can against his bruised cheekbone before taking a swig from it.

"So, what was that all about?" Andy inquired.

Aiden sighed. "I presume you know what the word 'gay' means?"

"Yeah. Sure," replied Andy matter-of-factly. "It's a guy who likes a guy. Or a girl who likes a girl."

"Right," said Aiden. "Well, that's me. I've found somebody I really like, and it's not a girl. His name is Roger."

"So, what's that got to do with those guys?" Andy asked, gesturing toward the street where the bullies had disappeared. "Why would they bash your head in for it?"

"Same reason you get your head bashed in for being Neanderthal," replied Aiden, pressing the soda pop can against his cheekbone again. They exchanged smiles: Andy's wide, toothy grin opposite Aiden's narrow face. They looked nothing alike, and yet at this moment they were unmistakably brothers. They sat there for a few minutes watching the sun dip below the treetops until Aiden asked, "Is anything wrong?"

"No, I was just thinking," Andy answered. "I always figured you'd be the one to get married and give Mom and Dad grandchildren, but I suppose if you're gay, that's not going to happen."

"No, not unless I choose adoption," answered Aiden.

"Or technology," grinned Andy. "Remember, you and I both came from the fertility lab."

"I hadn't thought of that," Aiden replied, "but I suppose it's an option."

"Just don't bring home any Neanderthals!" said Andy with a laugh.

Aiden smiled. "I could do worse. What about you? Don't you want kids?"

Andy shook his head firmly. "Not Neanderthal kids. I just learned how vasectomies work, and I'm planning to get one as soon as I turn 18. I'm okay with who I am now, but I don't want to produce more Neanderthals.

"One of me is enough," he grinned.

# CHAPTER 20: LIMITS AND OPTIONS

A few weeks into 9th grade algebra, Andy concluded that he had reached the limit of his progress on the higher-math-related subjects. This time, it wasn't lack of motivation; testing confirmed Andy's conclusions, and I recorded all of the test results for my data collection. At the time, the conclusion didn't bother Andy a bit, and he joked that he had "reached the ceiling of my cranium." With his academic advisors, he decided that beginning in 10th grade he would take half of his classes at the high school and half at the Vocational/Technical Center (VoTec) where he would study small engine mechanics. It was a choice that excited Andy, but it wouldn't happen until next year sometime. Meanwhile, he focused on his Scout projects and his other school subjects, since there was nothing about being Neanderthal that would give him an excuse to get out of his social studies, basic science, and language arts classes.

After the school year drew to a close and he knew he would be entering high school the next year, Andy became more concerned about his appearance. There would be two junior high schools funneling into his high school, so he would be in classes with students he'd never met before, and he wanted to look as "normal" as possible. He began the summer by consulting with Aiden about his hair. Andy had tried all kinds of hair styles, including pony-tailed and man-bun, and had even considered a bald look until he was shown a picture of a Neanderthal skull. So far, he had mostly stuck with a shoulder-length style that resembled Weird Al Yankovic, but it wasn't very flattering on Andy. Aiden helped him select a shorter style in which his curly red hair was layered into wavy strands that covered his forehead, the tips of his ears, and the back of his hairline. He liked the lighter feel of it. Aiden even put some lighter-color streaks in the hair, "just to add some depth."

"Do you think they'll call me a pansy?" joked Andy.

"Let them try," replied Aiden with a laugh.

Now that he had nearly reached physical maturity, Andy was also concerned about his protruding brow and exceptionally large nose, so early that summer he opted for cosmetic surgery to slightly reduce them. The brow surgery was the worst, because the surgeon had to remove a fair amount of bone from beneath the flesh. Andy spent two weeks with ice packs on his forehead, but said it would be worth it if he could get rid of his "built-in visor." Then he got some liposuction on his belly fat, which was another Neanderthal trait. He still looked Neanderthal, but somewhat less pronounced. He also decided that wrap-around sunglasses and a hat with a narrow brim were good ideas when he was in public so he wouldn't be too noticeable, especially to the media.

The new look gave Andy confidence, but he wouldn't be able to spend the summer staring in the mirror. There were Scout camp and guitar lessons, and his mother even enrolled him in an art class. His thick, muscular hands weren't great for drawing fine details like the hairs in a lion's mane, but he turned out to be pretty good at broad-brush paintings like sunsets over water. Besides, he liked the fact that those were pictures of nature.

When he wasn't at camp or classes, Andy's mother, always the English teacher, insisted that he continue his reading and writing skills. The reading part wasn't difficult: he loved the Harry Potter books. Writing, either on paper or computer, was of less interest to Andy, but Alicia was a firm believer that few things in life are more important than communication. Throughout his life, she said, he would have not only the media to deal with but also friends, family, co-workers, professionals, etc., and he would need to communicate intelligently with all of them, both verbally and in writing.

"But what if I'm not intelligent?" quipped Andy with a grin.

Without missing a beat, Alicia replied, "Then write about it."

# CHAPTER 21: ME AGAIN

Okay, it's me again: Larry. For the last several chapters, I haven't mentioned myself much because this is Andy's story, and I didn't want to interrupt it. So let me go back a bit and update you on what's been happening in my life.

After finishing my master's degree, I was able to get an office job with the university. It's not the greatest job, but it's in the archaeology department, so it allows me to stay up-to-date on what's happening in my field and to continue with my research in my off hours. I stay in touch with Louis, but he is now a full professor at a university on the west coast, in other words, as far away as he could possibly get from Pine State University and the controversies that surround it. He also gets the opportunity to travel the world looking for excavation sites, a job which, I must confess, I envy.

Of course, another benefit of my job is that it allows me to stay near Andy and his family. Yes, I'm observing him, but he's also a part of me, and I have no desire to completely let go of that, at least not yet.

During Andy's early years, he was observed and assisted by a variety of specialists from the university, one of whom was Beth, a psychologist specializing in children and families. Whenever Andy or his family was struggling, Beth was there with compassion and insight. I couldn't help being impressed by her ability to guide people in ways that never came across as condescending or judgmental. Oh, I'm sure she could be a really good bad guy when the occasion called for it, but at the Neill house, it never did. Simply offering suggestions or easing their anxiety was sufficient.

In my earlier years, my attraction to females came from the vantage point of me as a charming adventurer and the lady as a strikingly beautiful creature with a wouldn't-you-like-to-know look in her eyes. None of those factors were present here, yet I found myself missing Beth on the days when she wasn't nearby, and wanting to tell her every bit of news in my life when she was. I had to control that second response because I didn't want her to think I was using her as a free therapist, so I tried to keep our relationship as professional as possible. Besides, breaking that professional boundary could have gotten me fired in an instant.

It was Alicia who came to my rescue after seeing my disappointment on a day when Beth wasn't at Ivy House. Alicia approached Beth the next time she saw her and commented that Beth and I seemed to get along quite well together. When Beth smiled, Alicia asked, "Theoretically, hypothetically, how would you react if he asked you for a date?"

Beth replied, "Theoretically, hypothetically, I'd ask him what took him so long."

So, as Andy completed his 9th grade year, Beth and I had been married for eleven years, and our two daughters were six and eight years old.

None of that stopped us from remaining in almost constant contact with Andy and his family, as you will see in the next few chapters.

Read on.

# CHAPTER 22: HIGH SCHOOL

I guess it's common for kids in their mid-teens to go through a resentful stage. I know I did, and Beth tells me that she did, too, although I find that hard to imagine. For Andy, it happened shortly after he began 10th grade.

The school year had started out great. The high school was a bit confusing but also exciting, and Andy felt energized by it. Within a few weeks he even noticed that some girls, three girls in particular, were especially interested in him. He was flattered by their attention, and he hoped it was due to his new look, but he was also a bit confused because these were girls he had never met before. So what was the attraction? Were they charmed by his smile, by his jokes, by his muscles? He didn't know, but the girls were definitely flirting with him and even appearing to compete with each other for his attention. Whatever the reason, it bolstered his ego considerably.

Shortly after that, Alicia called me to say that the school principal had stopped by her classroom after hours to warn her about some "predatory girls" who were following Andy.

"Predatory girls?" I asked, secretly wondering where such girls had been when I was in high school.

"Yes," continued Alicia. They call themselves 'The Scorekeepers,' and they give themselves points for having slept with the captain of the football team, or the whole football team, or whatever. Word in the school right now is that they've got their sights set on 'the cave man.' Oh, and there were several boys in on it, too, placing bets on the girls' success or failure."

I felt sick. I've known plenty of males like that, and someday soon I would need to warn my daughters about them, but I'd never heard of it in girls. I thanked Alicia for letting me know and asked her to keep me informed, which she did.

Arnie was elected to give the news to Andy, and when he did, the result wasn't pretty. Andy slammed his books to the floor and threw up his hands in frustration. "Of course! I should have known. Why would I have ever thought that a girl – *any* girl - would actually choose to be with me?"

He sobbed as his anger began to build. "I'm just some prehistoric creature for people to laugh at, and beat up, and place bets on! I'm a Neanderthal freak in a *Homo sapiens* world, and that's never, never, never going to change!"

Then he turned his anger toward his parents (and me, although I wasn't present) for the fact that he'd ever even been brought into this world in the first place. He went into his bedroom and slammed the door. Alicia could hear loud sobs that sounded more like screams. When she brought him the traditional ice

cream with pineapple topping, he threw it across the
room.

For Andy, this wasn't just a fit of temper or teenage
angst, and it wasn't just about the embarrassment of
being mocked. He described it to Beth a few weeks
later as overwhelming grief. It was the painful
realization that he probably would never have the type
of companionship that he so desperately wanted. To
his peers, he would always be mostly a novelty. He
envisioned a lonely future in which he spent his days
repairing an endless stream of broken lawn mowers
and snow blowers in a dingy garage, returning to an
empty apartment at night.

The ice cream bowl was plastic, so it didn't break,
but the ice cream and topping splattered across the
hardwood floor and the plastered walls of Andy's'
room. Alicia ducked out in a hurry. She wasn't afraid
of her son, although she logically could have been.
Although Andy was emotionally and socially only 15,
he was a nearly full-grown Neanderthal man with
enough strength to do some serious household damage
if he wanted to. But she knew that wasn't what he
wanted, and besides, Arnie was there and would have
found a way to stop him if he'd gone too far. Instead,
Alicia and Arnie sat on the sofa together, listening in
agony to the sobbing behind the door. After a while,
Andy emerged, his face red from crying, and ducked
into the kitchen, where he grabbed a roll of paper
towels and a basin of water before returning to his

bedroom. When Arnie checked on him later that evening, he was sleeping, and the ice cream had been cleaned up. Arnie picked up the basin and quietly left the room. Considering the amount of ice cream that Alicia usually put into a bowl, there actually wasn't much in the basin. It appeared that Andy might have plopped the largest scoops back into the bowl and eaten them. Arnie managed a weak smile. Andy was still Andy, and he wasn't going to let good ice cream go to waste.

The next morning, Andy found a large note pushed under his door. It read, "We're sorry it's so hard right now. You deserve better. Please know that we love you, and that it will get better."

Andy returned to school the next day, and Beth talked with him on several occasions, but it would be several weeks before he was back to normal. His facial expression at school and at home was stone-faced. His grades dropped and he didn't care. He wouldn't touch his guitar. He resented everything and everyone.

After about three weeks of this, Alicia stood in front of him in the kitchen and softly said, "You have the right to be miserable if you want to. But you do not have the right to make the whole family miserable." Then she turned and went to sit in the living room with Arnie.

As bitter as he was, Andy knew she had a point. Besides, the prolonged resentment was getting old, even for him. He kind of missed the days when he was happier, and he wanted to feel that way again. He just wasn't sure whether it was possible.

To make things worse, Alicia's father, Jim Andrews, had recently passed away. "Grandpa Jim" had been the first person to celebrate his Neanderthal grandson, and Andy felt the loss deeply. But he knew that Alicia was struggling, too, especially as she tried to deal with her own mother's grief.

In his next visit with Beth, Andy wondered what had become of his old self, the little boy who'd been known for his big smile. Was that kid just naïve? Would he struggle forever with being the subject of ridicule?

Gradually, it did get better. Some of Andy's classes were interesting, and he began to come out of himself a bit. His social studies class showed films of people in third world countries facing starvation and war, which kind of put his own problems in perspective. He actually excelled in small engine repair and was making some friends in that class, and he continued his scouting activities.

Something else made a difference, too. One autumn day, Andy's biology teacher offered the students an unusual option: A landowner outside of town had died and left acres of rural land to the school system to be used as income property. There were stands of pine trees on the land, planted in rows and eventually destined to be harvested for lumber. For now though, the trees were about 30 feet tall and needed to be trimmed. The teacher drew a sketch of a row of pine trees on the blackboard, showing how, as the trees grow taller, the lower branches get shaded out and die. It's a natural process, but it leaves the lower trunk of the tree covered in stubby dead branches. As the tree grows, the trunk will grow around those dead branches, creating knots in the wood and diminishing the strength and value of the lumber. So, the students, if they wanted to, could be excused from their other classes to spend one day with hand saws and pole saws cutting off the dead branches.

No student was required to participate. Some in the hallways grumbled that they weren't interested in providing free labor for the school, but to Andy, this would be a welcome escape from the classroom. When he and the busload of students arrived at the stand of pine trees, Andy felt more alive than he had in months or years or perhaps ever. The fresh autumn breezes and the scent of the pine trees invigorated him. There were hundreds of trees and no hope of getting them all trimmed in one day, but for Andy, it wouldn't be for lack of trying. To his surprise, some of the girls were just as excited as he was about the project. They all worked together, exchanging saws and even laughing when it rained for a short time. At the end of the day, Andy's arms were tired and his neck was cramped from looking up, but he felt as if he had actually accomplished something. The next day, the teacher complimented several students, including Andy, for their work.

Later, Andy talked with Beth and me about it. Was it his Neanderthal heritage that made him so much more comfortable outdoors, or was it just him? Beth told him that there was no way to know for sure. Yes, genetics make a difference. Take, for example, a domestic rabbit and a wild rabbit. Put them in cages, and the domestic rabbit will be fine, while the wild rabbit may die trying to escape. But it's not just genetics, either. Plenty of *Homo sapiens* are much more comfortable working outdoors than in an office or a factory. In the end, it doesn't matter why. What matters is finding an environment that works for you.

After his sophomore year drew to a close, Andy got another chance to work outdoors as he organized and completed his Eagle Scout project, a foot bridge on the Pine Creek Hiking Trail. Again, he felt a sense of having accomplished something tangible.

That summer brought something else that mattered to him. It didn't have much to do with the outdoors, but it had plenty to do with freedom: Andy got his driver's license. He felt as if his life was getting back on track.

~~~

During his Junior year, Andy focused on his studies, his athletics (his dad, after all, was still the athletic director, so some sort of physical training was inevitable) and his small engine mechanics. In addition, he took a deeper interest in his Neanderthal heritage. Being Neanderthal was something he had generally accepted and occasionally resented, but he had never really studied it until now. He started spending many hours with me, wanting to learn everything I knew about Neanderthals and especially about the person he called his clone father, Glacier Pete.

The subject seemed to have a powerful impact on him. As Christmas and his 17th birthday approached, Andy asked his parents for cash instead of gifts. They assumed he wanted to put the money toward a used car, but instead, he announced that at the end of the school year he wanted to fly to Europe and visit the museum where Glacier Pete was displayed in a freezer. Arnie and Alicia weren't sure what to make of the request, but Beth said that it would probably be good for Andy, so they made flight arrangements for the family.

Arnie also arranged for Andy to get a summer job at a local park, mowing lawns and weeding gardens. It would be menial work, but it would allow him to spend some time outdoors, and some time working with the guy who repaired the mowers and tractors. As summer jobs go, it would be a win-win for Andy.

However, that would only happen after Andy returned from his visit to the museum.

# CHAPTER 23: THE MUSEUM TRIP

Aiden wasn't able to come along, but Alicia and Arnie accompanied Andy on the flight, and so did Beth and I and Louis, whom I hadn't seen in person for a couple of years. I showed Andy the photographs (not the artist's rendition but the real photographs) of Glacier Pete so he could be somewhat prepared for what he was about to see. On the plane, we discussed Pete in as much detail as possible. I was doing my best to prepare Andy, but I was also preparing myself, since I had not seen Pete since the day we discovered him.

The press was aware of our visit, but the museum allowed only a select few reporters and photographers in the room for the visit. The privacy laws of that country must have been a bit stronger than ours, because the reporters stayed off to the side of the room, which we all appreciated.

The room itself was a large, high-ceilinged, typical museum room. Neanderthal bones, tools, and other artifacts were displayed in glass cases along the walls. In the center of the room, in a horizontal freezer that looked like a thick glass showcase, was Glacier Pete. Andy took off his hat and held onto my arm as we approached him. The room was completely silent.

"It feels kind of strange. Weird," Andy said quietly, as he looked carefully at Pete. "He looks like me, but he's so… so…"

"Dead?" I volunteered.

"Yeah, something like that," whispered Andy. "I mean, in some ways he's so much like me that it's almost creepy. When I look at the texture of his hair and the shape of his hands, it's like I'm looking at myself. But he also looks pretty awful."

I had to agree with that. I had some vague recollection and several photos of what Glacier Pete looked like when I first saw him, but 18 years at the museum had left his skin looking dry and grainy, in spite of the carefully controlled climate in the freezer that had become his resting place.

Trying to make conversation, Andy whispered, "The sign says he was 5"6" tall, but I'm over 5'7". If we're genetically identical, how is that possible?"

"I'm not sure," I answered. "Probably nutritional and environmental differences."

"He's thinner than me, too, but that's definitely nutritional," added Andy with a tone of sadness. "I can't help thinking of all the foods I like that he'll never be able to taste, and the struggles he must have endured just to survive. He wasn't much older than me when he died, was he?"

"We think he was about 25, give or take a couple of years," I answered.

Andy handed me his hat and leaned over the display case. Although the sign said "Do Not Touch," he laid his hand on the case. The museum staff must have foreseen this, because although they watched from a few feet away, no alarms sounded and no one intervened. A few cameras clicked.

Then, slowly, Andy placed both hands on the case, and then laid his cheek on the glass. His eyes closed, in what was obviously an emotional moment. More cameras clicked.

When Andy stood up, he brushed tears from his eyes and stepped away from the display case, making room for his parents and Louis to get a better view.

"Would you like to tell us what you're feeling?" asked a reporter somewhat timidly.

Andy shook his head. "Not right now. I'll give you a statement in a few days."

As Andy and I stood at the side of the room, Louis tapped me on the shoulder, pointed across the room, and said, "Is that who I think it is?"

Oh, my God, yes, it was! She was standing quietly in the shadows, dressed in a dark business suit, but there was no mistaking Emilie. I asked Andy whether he was ready to add another emotional moment to the one he had just experienced. He had been informed of the role played by Emilie, but he never expected to meet her.

"What would I say?" he asked me.

"I don't know. I wasn't expecting this either," I said, assuring him that this was not a set-up. "But she did play a role in your existence. A pretty big role, actually."

Without another word, Andy stood up straight, walked across the room and shook Emilie's hand. I don't know everything that he said to her, but I heard the words, "Thank you" before he returned to his family.

As Emilie left the room, she turned for a moment, looked at me, and flashed a slight smile and a quick, but definite, wink.

Yes!!! I wasn't imagining it now, and I hadn't imagined it 18 years earlier. It really had been Emilie who had left the door to the clinic unlocked so I could use the freezer. A portion of the guilt that I had been carrying for all those years vanished in that moment.

~~~

The next day, Louis and I and the Neill family traveled to the glacier, or what was left of it, where we had found Glacier Pete. Louis and I were mostly fixated on how much deeper the valley had become as the ice melted, and I was glad it hadn't been that deep when Louis slipped down the rock face back then. But for Andy it was another emotional moment.

"He doesn't belong in that freezer," Andy blurted out, shaking his head. "I know that if he'd been left here, he would have been eaten by scavengers or something, and that would have been awful, but there's something even more awful about him being stuck in that freezer forever with an endless stream of tourists gawking at him. How long are they going to keep him there? Another twenty years? A hundred years? When does it end?"

He stopped to take a breath and then continued. "Why can't he have a normal burial and service and marker like we had for Grandpa Jim? Heck, even Gus got his ashes spread in the woods and a rock in his honor! So what does my clone father get? Eternity in a freezer? It's just wrong!"

The rest of us just looked at each other. It was Arnie who finally said, "If you feel that way, then maybe you should make a case for it."

"Why would anyone care what I think?" asked Andy in a bitter tone.

"Well, a case could be made that you are his next of kin," continued Arnie, who apparently had considered this possibility before the rest of us thought of it. "You'll be presenting a statement to the press after you get home, and if you think your Neanderthal relative shouldn't be in a freezer as a tourist attraction, then say so. I can't guarantee that it will change anything, but you definitely have a right to be heard."

~~~

When he returned to Michigan, Andy wrote and submitted his press statement and then retreated to his summer job with the county parks system, where he could focus on pulling weeds and cutting brush. He had long since learned to let the media do what media does, and just stay out of the line of fire, even though, in this case, he was the one who had fired the first shot. It was a delightfully devious move, and I rather admired him for it.

Social media blew up, as petitions were circulated on both sides. One side petitioned to "Preserve Glacier Pete for the People," while another side petitioned to "Free Glacier Pete from the Freezer." But the petitions would make little difference. In the end, this would be a battle of legalities and custody. Arnie had been prepared to hire a lawyer, but another group stepped in and furnished their own attorneys.

The museum claimed outrage that Andy would repay their hospitality by trying to steal their prize specimen. However, behind closed doors their own cryogenics specialists were begging them to view this as an opportunity to back out of an unsustainable situation. I hadn't been imagining it when I noticed Glacier Pete's grainy skin, and his experts were aware of it, too. Within a few years he probably wouldn't have any skin at all, and the curators would be faced with grim decisions. Andy was providing them with a convenient exit.

Meanwhile, attorneys battled over who had legal rights to the corpse. The museum investors reminded everyone that Glacier Pete wasn't really Andy's "father." But the opposing side said that technically he was Andy's identical twin, which was even worse for the museum's case. Neither side wanted a public trial, although it would likely have worked to Andy's advantage.

When it became clear that the judgment would probably be in Andy's favor, the museum negotiated a deal. On Andy's 18th birthday, which was five months away in February, he would be given custody of Glacier Pete. Meanwhile, the museum would make a mold of the corpse so that they could create an exact replica for their display, which was what their cryogenics experts had been recommending for the last several years anyway. And, in a nod to archaeologists who wanted to study Pete, an autopsy would be permitted before the remains would be released for burial or cremation.

Andy agreed, and the papers were signed.

# PART 3: ONWARD

# CHAPTER 24: THE SECOND TRIP

Andy's work with the county parks system had been a good match, so when he returned to school for his Senior year, he added whatever classes he could find in nature studies, as well as continuing his mechanics classes. He had only two other required classes for graduation, and they weren't difficult, so he was able to make the most of the classes that really mattered to him.

He had planned to wait until spring break to make the trip to claim custody of Glacier Pete's remains, but this was 2020, and by early February, COVID-19 loomed on the horizon. Andy was advised to make his trip as soon as possible, and even then he might not be able to book a flight. The local branch of an international corporation stepped in with a solution: They had a few executives who needed to make last minute trips to Europe before everything shut down, so Andy and his guests would be welcome to accompany them on the corporate jet. Arnie and Alicia wouldn't be able to leave their teaching jobs, so Louis and I accompanied Andy.

We left Michigan the day after Andy's 18th birthday, and the following day, in a small ceremony at the museum, he accepted custody papers for Pete's remains. This time, Andy didn't actually see the corpse because it was already being defrosted for the autopsy, which Louis and I observed the next day while Andy was given a tour of the city. Louis and a few other researchers were able to collect additional tissue samples for study, this time without any secrecy required. Andy had custody of the corpse, and he permitted it, as long as the samples never got anywhere near a reproductive clinic.

Andy had decided that burial was not a good option for Pete because some idiot might try to dig him up, so all three of us toured the area for the next two days until the cremation had been completed.

With the box of ashes in hand, we were driven to Glacier Peaks, where Andy scattered Pete's ashes on the vegetation-covered southern slope of the mountain. A memorial marker had been placed on the lawn near the parking area, so Andy and a local preacher stood next to it and spoke a few words honoring Pete's life.

This time, Andy wasn't particularly emotional about the trip. The remains of his "Clone Father" had been freed from the freezer and recognized in a memorial service, and that was what mattered to him. With the ceremonies completed, Andy was ready to go home. But COVID-19 was gaining ground, and vaccinations wouldn't be available for another year, so before he left Europe, Andy's doctors recommended that he stay as far away from civilization as possible. Their concern was that a Neanderthal immune system might not be effective against the disease, a problem they were already seeing in other subgroups such as the Native American community. Andy's mother advised him not to take any chances.

Andy told her that one of the cottages in Ontario might be an option, since electrical wiring and plumbing had been installed a few years earlier, but he didn't want to miss school and put his graduation at risk. Alicia explained that the school would soon be switching to all-virtual classes anyway, so it wouldn't matter where he stayed. She just wanted him to be safe.

Louis and I had to get back to the USA before the borders closed, so the corporate plane dropped Andy off alone at the airport in snowy Sudbury, Ontario, which didn't seem to bother him a bit. Consulting with his dad by cell phone, Andy bought a six-year-old pickup truck, which he loaded with supplies and drove south to the cottage.

After arranging for a satellite dish to be installed at the cottage for internet service, Andy spent his days alternating between online classes, ice fishing from the dock, cutting firewood, and hiking along the rocky banks of the Magnetawan. In one of his emails to me, he joked that he was glad it was too early in the season for tourists, because if anyone saw him, with his broad build and rough features, roaming through the snowy woods, they would probably think they were seeing Bigfoot. I felt a bit relieved knowing that he hadn't lost his sense of humor.

Sitting by the fireside at night, Andy didn't feel as if he had lost anything.  He wouldn't want to be away from his family forever, but, for now, he was enjoying the wilderness as well as the luxuries that his ancestors never had.

It was the best of both worlds.

# CHAPTER 25: THE PARK MANAGERS

After about two weeks, Andy realized he needed more supplies.  He was running out of a few things, plus his original list had been thrown together somewhat hastily.  There were probably smaller towns where he could have gotten the basics, but he decided to grab his mask and his truck and make the drive to Sudbury again, where he knew there was a wilderness supply store.

To most of us the mask-wearing requirement of that time was somewhat of an inconvenience, but to Andy it was a hidden blessing.  It covered his nose, mouth, and chin, which were his most obvious Neanderthal features.  Wearing a hat and a mask, Andy could move among the general population without looking noticeably different from everyone else.

At the wilderness supply store Andy joined a conversation between the owner and one of the regular customers, a tall man named Gordon whose wavy greying hair and wrinkled forehead somehow accentuated his well-used muscles.  Gordon and his indigenous wife, Sunbeam, usually called Sunny, served as caretakers for a large provincial park some distance east of Sudbury.  That gave Andy an opportunity to open up about his own interest in park maintenance: his small engine repair classes as well as his summer of work with the county parks system, his pine-tree pruning excursion, and the foot bridge that he had built as his Eagle Scout project. As he told the stories, he realized how boyish they sounded, but Gordon nodded and seemed genuinely impressed. He immediately offered Andy a job.

Gordon explained that at this time of year (it was mid-March) most areas of the park were still closed because winter lingers into April in Sudbury, and this year the park probably would remain closed throughout much of the season due to COVID. But the province of Ontario was wise enough to recognize that this would be a good opportunity for some maintenance and upgrades.

Andy was excited about the offer but asked to discuss it in a bit more detail with Gordon outside of the store. Gordon recommended a little-known diner where they could get a meal without much risk of being exposed to COVID, so they placed their food order through a Plexiglas window at the counter and then found a booth in the back where they could talk privately. Gordon assumed that Andy wanted to ask how much the job paid and what hours he would be expected to work, but Andy wasn't concerned about that. He needed to let Gordon know what he was getting himself into.

First, Andy explained that he still had three more months of online high school classes to complete. That surprised Gordon a bit, since Andy looked more like a guy in his early 20s (a really muscular guy, as Gordon could see when Andy removed his jacket.) But Gordon said that the cabin where Andy would be staying had a good internet system, which he was welcome to use to complete his classes. He just needed to promise to do the park's work whenever possible.

Then Andy had to ask the question that he hated so much: Did Gordon recall hearing about a kid who had been born in Michigan back in 2002 from a Neanderthal embryo? Gordon thought for a moment and said yes, he recalled reading about that.

"Well, I'm that kid," said Andy, removing his mask as the food arrived. "And back in the states it came with a lot of unwanted publicity. I thought you had a right to know about it."

Again, Gordon looked thoughtful, nodding his head. "I don't think it will be a big problem here," he said. "We get a lot of rugged-looking types around here. Sometimes we have events like lumberjack contests. And our law enforcement officers generally make sure people respect each other's privacy. I think we can deal with it."

They shook hands, and Andy thanked Gordon profusely. Gordon just smiled, noticing that Andy had never even asked how much the job pays.

Gordon and Sunbeam owned an older two-story house and three cabins just outside the front entrance to the park, so Andy moved his belongings from the cottage on the Magnetawan to one of the cabins.

Whenever he wasn't in a virtual classroom, he was
cutting brush and branches along the hiking trails,
laying new railroad ties around the edges of the
campsites, shoveling bark chips, repairing fences and
picnic tables, and preparing the lawn tractors and
mowers for the upcoming season. (For a few weeks,
my email inbox was flooded with pictures and videos of
the park and every project that Andy and Gordon
worked on.) When they completed a project, Gordon
sometimes took Andy for a walk through the park,
showing him how to identify different species of trees
by their bark and twigs when they had no leaves.

"Robin's going to thank me for hiring you," grinned
Gordon. "Otherwise a lot of this work would have
fallen on her when she gets home from college. She's
good at it, but she can always use more help."

Gordon had mentioned his daughter, Robin, before.
He said that she was currently finishing up a two-year
course of study in forestry and natural resources at
Michigan State University. Andy said it was a
curriculum that interested him, too, and he thought of
the irony that Robin was in Michigan and he was in
Ontario, each of them stranded away from their
families.

~~~

In the evenings, Andy often called home. On one
occasion his parents were out buying groceries, so
Aiden answered the phone, which was fine with Andy
because they hadn't had a chance to talk for a while.

Aiden was finishing up his third year at Pine State University and, like Andy, was doing most of his classroom work online.

It occurred to Andy that he had been so preoccupied with his own events during the last several months that he hadn't really been keeping up on what was happening in Aiden's life. So he took this opportunity to ask, and Aiden was more than willing to share. Aiden said that he was finding a direction for his career, and that Andy's experiences had played a role in it.

"*My* experiences?" asked Andy.

"Yes, both of us, actually," explained Aiden. "I watched you get bullied in school and demonized by the media for being Neanderthal. And then I was the one who got bullied and demonized for being a gay man. So, I started noticing other people who were facing the same kinds of discrimination. Racial minorities. Immigrants. Persons with disabilities. The list goes on. And you and I had advantages that most of those people never get."

Aiden sighed and then continued, "I decided I wanted to make a difference. So I'm in a pre-law curriculum and I plan to specialize in protecting the rights of disadvantaged groups and individuals."

"Aiden, that's awesome!" exclaimed Andy.

"Thanks," replied Aiden. "I'll be getting some practice pretty soon. I've signed up for an internship this summer with a diversity non-profit."

"You're definitely the right guy for the job," assured Andy.

"I hope so," answered Aiden with some uncertainty in his voice. Changing the subject, he added, "By the way, Roger and I broke up."

"Oh, gee," said Andy in a tone that failed miserably in concealing his relief. Trying to backtrack, he added, "I'm really sorry."

"It's okay," replied Aiden. "Everybody kept telling me that he was the wrong guy for me, but it took me a while to figure it out."

"You deserve better. You'll find better," reassured Andy.

After a moment, Aiden said, "Speaking of relationships, I remember you mentioning on a few occasions that you planned to get a vasectomy. Is that still your plan?"

"Yes, definitely," Andy affirmed. "I'm 18 now, so it's on my short list."

"Well, that's why I brought it up," explained Aiden. "If you're going to be in Canada for a while, you might want to take advantage of your dual citizenship and get it done there. The minimum age for the procedure in Ontario is 18. In Michigan, it's 21."

"*Twenty one*?" yelped Andy. "I didn't know that. Yes, I'll definitely get it done here, then, and soon. Not that I have a need right now, but I just want to be assured that I'll never have to worry about bringing any more accidental Neanderthals into the world. It's something that nobody else can understand. For me, it's peace of mind."

"I get it," replied Aiden.

Two weeks later, Andy paid a visit to a clinic in Sudbury and then sent Aiden an email saying only, "The Neanderthal polliwogs aren't swimming anymore." Aiden laughed. He really did get it.

# CHAPTER 26: GRADUATION AND PURPOSE

As graduation approached, Andy learned that it, too, would be virtual, which was a relief to him because the borders had been closed so he was now pretty much stuck in Canada. Ten days before graduation the school principal called Andy and asked whether he would like to present a short speech for the online ceremony.

Andy's stunned response was, "Why me?" He wasn't the valedictorian or the salutatorian, and he understood that a state legislator would be giving a speech.

"The state legislator got picked up on a drunk driving charge and is in jail," explained the principal. "So he's out of the picture. The staff and members of the student council decided that you are the closest thing this school has to a celebrity, plus they think you'll have something worthwhile to say. They unanimously decided that I should ask you." Then he added, "I think a certain English teacher would be proud."

Andy laughed, "Oh, so you're bringing Mom into it! Okay, now you're not playing fair. That's extortion!"

"Well, give it some thought anyway," said the principal.

Andy did consult with his mom, and his dad, and Aiden, and even me and Beth. Nobody helped him write the speech, but they did ask him a few key questions to help him zero in on what was important to him. Andy still had his doubts, but Aiden commented that since the ceremony was being held online, anyone who didn't want to listen to his speech could just turn off the volume. Although Aiden was clearly joking, Andy found it reassuring to know that he wouldn't be speaking before a captive audience.

When the day came, he was nervous but ready. Wearing his graduation cap and gown, he stood outdoors at a makeshift podium with a pine tree as his background and a smile on his face. Gordon and Sunbeam stood nearby for moral or technical support as he presented this speech:

>Teachers and fellow classmates, at the request of our erstwhile principal, I address you today, not as the class valedictorian or the class salutatorian, but as the class oddball.
>
>I guess most of you know my story: my DNA is over 40,000 years old. And it came together (accidentally I'm told) through technology that would have been unheard of a few decades ago. I don't think it's a stretch to say that I'm unique.
>
>And yet, I am no more unique than anyone else here. We all have DNA that dates back 40,000 years. It's just that yours has passed

through hundreds of generations of people who survived wars and famines and plagues, yet somehow managed to raise families throughout the challenges. And for their efforts, amazing improvements have been made: in medicine, technology, and even things like building construction. We don't live in caves anymore.

Our generation faces its own challenges. Today, we are separated from each other by a contagious disease. We have lost time together, and a few among us have lost loved ones. To those people, I offer my sincere condolences. To the rest of us, we will get through this, but we must get through it together. Our society gives a great deal of credit, maybe too much credit, to the competitive spirit, but it is the ***collective*** effort that allows humanity to persevere. Through cooperation, we can experience progress. Through kindness, we can experience joy.

But achieving cooperation requires more than warm, fuzzy thoughts. It also requires the knowledge and the will to resist the forces that come between us. There will always be individuals who stand to gain by dividing us into tribes and pitting one against another. Someone will always be ready to convince us that another person or group should be feared or mocked or destroyed. Someone will always be ready to bolster our egos by leading us to believe that only *our* race, *our* nation, or *our* species has the right to survive and thrive.

Every day, we are bombarded with vast quantities of information, misinformation, and intentional disinformation. Our goal must be to filter that information not by what we want to believe but by what constitutes the unvarnished truth.

Today, we have boundless resources for connecting with each other and for finding that truth. Please use those resources wisely. Humanity is enhanced by knowledge. Let it be the knowledge that helps us fight diseases and hunger rather than each other.

Be kind. Be wise. Be safe.

Thank you.


The principal was right. A certain English teacher was very proud.

~~~

Andy's speech made its way across the Internet and caught the attention of human rights groups across the country. But it was Aiden who called and asked Andy to serve as one of their advocates. By this time, Aiden was working as a pre-law intern, and his superiors agreed that they'd like to have Andy as one of their spokesmen. At first, Andy was reluctant, but after listening to their terms, he felt that he might be able to help. They didn't need or want him to leave his current job. They just wanted him to make occasional online or in-person appearances to reduce bullying and encourage inclusion.

Andy accepted their offer, not so much because he wanted to as because he needed to. He knew what it was like to be excluded, and he also knew that in spite of his painful experiences, there were others who experienced much worse. Yes, he was Neanderthal, but he understood that he was also the product of an extraordinary combination of resources: He had been given the benefit of every field of expertise that Pine State University had to offer, and he had been raised by two parents who were well-educated, financially secure, and experienced with children. He understood that too many children who are different have no such advantages, living in a world where they are financially as well as socially marginalized, and where they have few resources to help them.

Now Andy had the benefit, as well as the curse, of publicity, and it seemed only fair that he should use that podium to help others. It wouldn't take much of his time; he would still be mostly an employee of the parks department or whatever other job he might take in the future. But when he was called for an appearance, yes, he would answer.

# CHAPTER 27: ROBIN

Shortly after Andy's graduation, the caretakers' daughter, Robin, returned from her second year of college. Due to the COVID restrictions at that time, she had to isolate for 14 days, so Andy's first meeting with her was through a window. He stood outside her cabin wearing his mask, mostly to conceal his face, and talked with her on Gordon's phone, excitedly describing all of the projects that they had been working on for the last two months. Robin had heard quite a bit about Andy from Gordon, and was now seeing for herself what her dad meant when he described Andy's enthusiasm and said, "He kind of grows on you." She told Andy a little about the classes she'd been taking, and Andy said he hoped to take some of the same classes whenever he could get the opportunity.

Robin had her quarantine time calculated to the minute. As soon as it was over, she stepped into action alongside Andy, and he got his first opportunity to observe her in action. Again, Andy sent me lots of pictures and videos of the two of them working together. Appearance-wise, Robin was not fashion-model beautiful. She was short and stocky and she had her mother's high, wide cheekbones and wide nose. Those were features that Andy could relate to, but this young woman was all *Homo sapiens* with a quiet confidence to match.  Her long, wavy black hair was usually pulled straight back in a ponytail, swinging from side to side as she walked and worked.

She was energetic but not in the animated way that Andy was.  Her motions were steady and purposeful, and she had organization down to an art.   She was also remarkably intelligent.  She had been studying nature nearly all of her life, but also excelled at the more theoretical sciences such as physics and chemistry. She could easily have qualified for advanced degrees at MSU or any other college, but for now, she chose the short program so she could return to the parks system as quickly as possible.  In her words, "I have nothing to prove."

She had certainly impressed Andy.  In a Skype call to me, he said, "Larry, I hope you can meet Robin soon. She's just amazing!  She can even speak two different Native languages, as well as French!  I love listening to her when she's speaking to someone in French!"

I knew that feeling, and I had a pretty good idea that I'd be hearing a lot more about this young woman.

~~~

Robin worked side by side with Andy throughout the summer and started looking forward to his grin and his humor.  When the fall term would have started, vaccinations were still not yet available, so both Andy and Robin settled for taking whatever they could get in the way of online classes while they continued to work on the park upgrades.  Andy repaired the mechanical equipment, and they worked together with her father on the outdoor improvements, a job made easier by the fact that the camp was still mostly closed to tourists. In the evenings they would sometimes sit around a campfire, and Andy would play his guitar. He didn't have a singing voice but Robin and Gordon and Sunny did, so sometimes they'd sing along. But most of the time, they just listened to the strumming and watched the crackling flames.

Another project that had been ongoing during the summer was the construction of a new building at the park. For several decades there had been three picnic pavilions in the park, but Pavilion C, the one closest to the front office, rarely got used. Most people preferred to do their picnicking closer to the lake where the view was better. So Gordon hadn't been surprised when he got a message from the provincial park administrators instructing him to replace the old roofing on Pavilions A and B, but not C. What surprised him was the next paragraph: A construction crew would be sent in to dismantle Pavilion C, all except the big stone fireplace, and replace it with a log building to house a new nature center.

By autumn the building had been completed, but it was Gordon, Sunny, Robin, and Andy who would set up all of the displays. Sunny, whose artistic talents were well-known, created mural-sized photos and drawings to be hung on the walls. The other three set up carefully labeled displays of tree branches and leaves, insect collections, models of wildlife, and even a few aquariums and terrariums for temporary occupancy by live critters, although those wouldn't be inhabited until next spring. Having spent his share of time in museums, Andy had a few good suggestions for displaying the specimens. Above them they stretched a huge black tarp between the rafters, with lights above the tarp gleaming through tiny holes that the trio had drilled to replicate the constellations of stars.

In early December, Andy returned to Michigan to visit his family. The border was still closed to land travel but he learned of a loophole that allowed him to travel by air. Again, the corporate jet, which was making regular flights across the border anyway, allowed Andy to hitch a ride. The return to Michigan also allowed Andy to take some exams at MSU so he could get full credit for the fall classes that he'd been taking online. Some of the exams were held outdoors, where the professor walked the students around the campus and along the Red Cedar River, pointing to a tree or shrub and instructing the students to write the Latin name of the plant. Others were traditional exams held in shifts in half-empty classrooms where everyone wore masks.

Over the Christmas holiday, Andy chatted enthusiastically to his family about the park, his projects, his cabin, Gordon, Sunny, and, of course, Robin. Alicia was a bit surprised at how much her younger son had grown up in less than a year.

Physically he was slightly stronger and leaner, but the biggest differences were in his maturity and his confidence. However, there was also no mistaking the fact that Robin was behind much of his enthusiasm, and that worried Alicia a bit. All she could do was what any mother does: hope things worked out, and be there for him if they didn't.

Shortly after Christmas there were a couple of days when warm breezes blew in from the south and the temperature jumped into the mid-50s, so I was able to meet with Andy in the backyard of Ivy House for a long-awaited visit. With me he spoke more seriously about his feelings for Robin. He knew that Robin probably wouldn't be interested in a romantic relationship with him, so he wasn't about to ruin everything by bringing up the subject with her. All he knew for sure was that he was happier *with* her than without her, and he would do everything in his power to preserve the friendship and working relationship that they had.

"She's just such an amazing and interesting person!" he said. "I've learned so much from her and her dad, and I've had such great experiences that..." he stopped and took a deep breath, "even if the time comes, and it probably will, that she comes back from college with an engagement ring on her finger, I can't honestly say I'll have lost anything. Even if I transfer to a different park, Robin and Gordon and that park will always be a part of me, and I'll be prepared to move on to something new."

Andy's voice was cheerful, and I admired him for his determination to make the best of whatever life gave him. Yet I thought of Beth and my daughters, and I felt the sadness that Andy wouldn't allow himself to feel.

# CHAPTER 28: RETURN TO ONTARIO

Andy decided to stay in Michigan through the end of the spring 2021 semester. Actually, it was a decision made for him because Canada was getting pretty strict about its borders, and vaccinations would be available soon in Michigan, so he might as well wait it out.

He signed up for four classes that could be taken mostly online with occasional, mostly outdoor, visits to the MSU campus. In addition to the spring class on tree and shrub identification he signed up for classes on insects, soils, and herbaceous perennials.

By mid-May, with all four classes and both vaccinations behind him, Andy returned to Ontario. With vaccines beginning to roll out, the park would be open on a limited basis, so there was plenty of work to be done and he looked forward to working with Gordon and Robin again.

Aside from helping to set up the nature center, Sunny, Robin's mother, worked mostly behind the scenes. She ordered supplies, did the bookkeeping, checked campers in and out of the park, and handled all manner of requests from the park visitors. She had a bad knee from an injury years ago, so she couldn't do much of the physical work, but when she wasn't in the office she was on the golf cart greeting visitors and answering their questions, although there were fewer visitors this year.  There were always some park visitors who came just for the purpose of seeing Sunny when they arrived.  And now she had the nature center to attend to as well.  She kept it clean and gave visitors a uniquely indigenous perspective on the area's history.   And, in her spare time, she retired to her sewing room to work on a secret personal project that even Gordon didn't know about.

In addition to their maintenance work, Andy and Robin, and sometimes Gordon, led families on nature walks along some of the trails.  They pointed out specific plants and animals, and if there were children present, Andy would entertain them by grabbing onto a low tree limb and hoisting himself up on it, and then pretending to be a silly-looking bird sitting on the branch.  He even had a face mask shaped like a beak.  If a child got tired of walking, Andy would carry him or her on his shoulders or in a backpack carrier made for that use.  On one occasion he kicked off his work boots and jumped into a pond to help a kid catch a turtle, even though Andy knew the turtle would have to be returned to the pond as soon as the kids had gotten a chance to look it over.

The park had a playground too, and if Andy spotted children who had been brought to the park by their grandparents, he stopped his work to keep them occupied.  Robin would see him doing one of his tumbling runs on the lawn, or hanging from the jungle gym with giggling children clinging to both of his legs.

She sent me a video of him playing Nerf football with the kids just as I had done 15 years earlier at Ivy House. He had come to the conclusion that if his Neanderthal features were ridiculous, they might as well serve a purpose. He practiced in the mirror making goofy faces and he often tucked a tall weed into the band of his narrow-brimmed hat, having refused to switch over to the more commonly worn baseball cap.

One day, as Andy and Robin ate their lunches within sight of some playing children, Andy asked Robin whether she ever planned to have kids.

"Probably not. I enjoy working with kids, but I think reproduction is overrated," she replied with a grin. "Besides, the world already has over 7 billion people, which has created an environmental mess, so I'm not really interested in contributing to that."

She asked Andy how he felt about having kids, and he reminded her that he'd had a vasectomy. "The *Homo sapiens* can decide for themselves whether they want to reproduce, but I'm not bringing any Neanderthals into the world," he said with a shake of his head. "As I told my brother, one of me is enough."

"Maybe so, but I kind of like the one of you," Robin said with a smile.

~~~

Andy had planned to return to MSU for the fall 2021 term, but with the Delta variant sweeping through the world, he decided to stay in his remote corner of Canada again. His family agreed. The classes could wait, so he stayed to finish up the season with Robin and her family at the park.

Robin's degree and Gordon's accomplishments had not gone unnoticed by the Ontario Ministry of the Environment, Conservation and Parks. At the end of the season, Robin's father received a formal notice from the parks administration that beginning next spring he would be promoted to head of the western Ontario regional parks system. Although his residence near the park would remain his official address, he, and sometimes Sunny, would be traveling much of the time to assist and advise other park managers. At the same time, Robin received a notice saying that she would become the new official manager of her dad's park.

Andy called me that evening and said that when he congratulated Robin on her promotion, she responded with only a weak "Thanks." When he asked her whether she'd like to talk about it, she explained that it was a position she had wanted eventually, but not so soon. "I thought I'd be taking over the park in five years or so when my dad retires," she said. "That would have given me time to take more classes and learn more from Dad. And I thought Mom would still be here to help with the office work. With both of them on the road, I'm going to be flying solo sooner than I had intended, and I'm going to have to hire people to do the work that Mom and Dad did. It just feels kind of overwhelming."

Andy answered. "Well, I'll help in any way I can."

"I know you will," replied Robin. "And I know you can work independently. You have the ability to see what needs to be done and just do it. I can't tell you how much I appreciate that." Then she grinned and said, "Please don't run off to Michigan anytime soon!"

"Don't worry. I'm not going anywhere," replied Andy.

~~~

One evening I was surprised when my cellphone jingled and said: "Larry: you have a Skype call from Robin. Press to answer or decline." Of course, I answered, and Robin told me about her promotion, although I'd already heard about it from Andy. After a bit of light conversation she asked, somewhat awkwardly, "Is there anything I should know about Andy? I mean anything in his medical or legal history? Does he have a dark side? Now that I'm officially going to be his employer, I just want to make sure I know these things."

I wasn't quite sure why Robin was asking me these questions, since Andy had already passed a background check nearly a year-and-a-half earlier when he first started working there. Nevertheless, I assured her that he had no dark side, no criminal record, and no health problems that have shown up so far. Then I asked her whether she had seen any behaviors in Andy that led to these concerns.

"No, none at all!" she blurted out in a baffled tone of voice. "He's hardworking and delightful to talk to, and he's great with the campers and kids. He's almost too good to be true, and that always brings up questions for me."

She stopped for a moment before resuming her rambling monologue. "I mean, yes, he's Neanderthal, but how much does it matter that he wouldn't pass a calculus test? If the campers can trust him, I guess I can, too, right? I've met guys who had a lot more cave man mentality than he does. And I really don't care what anyone else thinks. I have nothing to prove." Then she quickly thanked me for my time and said she had to go.

I turned to Beth, who had overheard the one-sided conversation, and asked, "Am I crazy, or was she evaluating him for more than just parks work?"

"Oh, you're crazy," Beth replied with a smile, "but not about that."

~~~

If Robin had feelings for Andy, she wasn't talking about them yet, but her parents were beginning to notice. As Gordon and Sunbeam stood near the front office, they watched Robin giggling when Andy spoke, grabbing his arm to show him something of interest, and giving him a one-arm hug when a job was completed to their satisfaction. It wasn't much, but they knew it was real.

Sunny spent a little extra time in her sewing room that evening.

# CHAPTER 29: A FAMILY'S LOSS

As the fall season rolled on, and so did Delta, Robin and Gordon and Andy worked on bringing the park's season to an end. Frosty nights brought the scent of autumn and an end to pesky mosquitoes, so Andy relished the peace and quiet of the park. Soon the trio would have to begin the leaf clean-up project, but first Andy got permission to take a short vacation to his family's cottage on the Magnetawan River. He would spend a couple of days fishing, and then drain the water pipes at the cottage and close it up for the winter. Robin stayed at the park.

Just as he was finishing up at the cottage, Andy got a text message from Robin. "What time do you expect to arrive?" she asked. "Leaving right now," answered Andy. "Okay, text me when you get here so we can meet in the nature center. We need to talk," she replied.

None of this made any sense to Andy. Robin had told him that he was welcome to take his time at the cottage, so what was the sudden rush? And "we need to talk" is almost never a good thing. Was it about him? During their few days apart had she decided that they should keep their distance? Was it something about his work? Or had something happened to Gordon or Sunbeam? Whatever it was, it couldn't be good. On his drive back to the park he called me on his cellphone to share his sense of impending doom. I asked him to tell me how it turned out, and he promised he would. When he got out of the truck, he stuffed some Kleenex in his pocket, not knowing for sure who would need them.

He found Robin sitting on a park bench inside the nature center, the late afternoon sun peeking into the window through the yellowing leaves. She was slouched over, rubbing her forehead with her thumb and fingertips. He took a seat at the other end of the bench and waited. Finally, she spoke.

"It looks as if we may need to rethink our decision not to raise kids," she said in a somber tone.

Andy thought, "We?" but he said nothing. Apparently, Robin was thinking the same thing, because she continued, "Well, actually I'm the one who has to rethink it, but it's definitely going to affect all of us."

"Maybe you should take me back to the beginning," said Andy, "because I think my Neanderthal brain missed something."

Robin sighed. "Do you remember my cousin Dawn and her husband Nighthawk? They're both First Nation, and they came to visit us from the reserve earlier this summer. Dawn is the daughter of my mom's older sister, Starlight."

"Oh, yes," said Andy. "I remember that visit. Dawn's husband goes by 'Hawk,' right? And they have two little kids, a toddler boy and a baby girl?" Andy remembered the visit well. It had been an outdoor visit, with everyone except the children wearing masks. Dawn looked a lot like Robin, and they got close to each other only long enough to pass the baby girl, Kayla, back and forth. But it was Hawk that Andy remembered best: he was tall and muscular, with a boyish grin and seemingly endless energy for playing with his three-year-old son, Kyle.

"They had to cut their visit short so Dawn could return to her job at the food processing plant. Unfortunately, when the Delta variant hit, it swept through the plant. Dawn caught it and brought it home. The kids just got sniffles, but Hawk got hit hard. He died within two weeks."

"He DIED?" gasped Andy.

"Yes. And after a month in the hospital, Dawn survived, but she's in rough shape. She has permanent lung damage and kidney damage. She's on supplemental oxygen and dialysis, and it takes most of her energy just to breathe. Her mother has to help her."

Andy was beginning to see where this was going, but he was still trying to grasp the fact that Hawk was dead. Andy had looked forward to becoming friends with Hawk, but this wasn't the moment for that conversation.

"Dawn can't take care of herself, much less her kids," continued Robin. "And her mother has all she can do to take care of herself and Dawn. The tribe was decimated by the outbreak, so they can't do much, either.

"Dawn wants to avoid relinquishing the kids for adoption or long-term foster care. She'd like them to be cared for by a relative so she can visit them whenever possible. That's where we come in."

"We?" asked Andy, this time accidentally letting the word slip out loud. "Are you saying that you want to raise the kids **with** me? Or do you just mean that it will affect me because I'll be working with you at the park?"

Robin rubbed her forehead again, took a deep breath, and then answered, "Either or both. Yes, this will affect you even if we're just co-workers and friends, and you have every right to limit it to that. I'll appreciate whatever help you're willing to give."

Then she took another deep breath and continued, "But your question was 'do I want to raise the kids *with* you,' and the reality is that I want to do everything with you. I miss you if you're gone for even a day. You're more than my helper and my friend, you're a big part of who I am and who I want to be. I've felt this way for months now, but I didn't say anything because I guess I didn't want either of us to get hurt."

With a sigh of frustration she added, "And whatever I say now, it's going to sound as if I'm saying it because this huge load has been dumped on me and I need help, which I do, but..." She brushed tears from her eyes, and Andy gave her a couple of the tissues from his pocket.

"So, exactly what is it that you want to say?" asked Andy.

Robin thought for a moment, took a deep breath, and answered, "That I love you. I've known it for quite a while now, but I wasn't ready to put it into words."

"Oh, I understand why you wouldn't have said anything earlier," answered Andy. "Those are powerful words, especially considering who I am. I'm not exactly the guy next door."

Robin laughed through her sniffling. "Yes, you are. Your cabin is right next to mine."

"Okay, good point. But you know what I mean. I come with a lot of baggage: genetic baggage, publicity baggage, you name it. Heck, I'm not even the same *species* as you... or any other girl that I would date, although they're not exactly lining up," he said, knowing that he was getting off topic.

"Their loss," sniffed Robin with a smile.

Andy continued, "You're brilliant, and you could have the smartest guy on the planet. I'm not sure you should be settling for me."

"I'm not settling," she answered. "I'm sitting next to the person I want to be with. But because I've waited so long to say anything, it sounds like I'm saying this for practical reasons. And, to be honest, the practical reasons are real, too. And I know I'm not making any sense."

Robin wiped her eyes again and shook her head. She was accustomed to doing things in a steady, methodical way, and keeping her life under control. Now everything was out of control.

"I can't think of anything you should have done differently," said Andy, moving a bit closer on the bench. "You wanted to take your time, and then this situation came along, and now we're dealing with a different reality. And yes, the practical stuff matters. I look at the things my parents do, and it's probably 90% practical stuff. But they support each other, even when they get stuck doing something completely unexpected and totally insane, like raising a Neanderthal kid!"

"That's why I love you so much," smiled Robin, blowing her nose. She stood up and walked across the room to throw away the tissue and get a squirt of hand sanitizer. Andy followed her, and they stood facing each other.

"I hope you know that I love you, too," ventured Andy.

"I thought you did. I hoped you did. But I didn't want to assume anything," smiled Robin, laying her arm on his left shoulder.

"Well, you can go ahead and assume now," grinned Andy.

Then he put his left arm around her back and leaned forward with a big smile on his face. Robin thought he might be leaning in for a kiss, and she hoped he wasn't because her face was literally a hot mess.

But, instead, he bent quickly to about waist height and slipped his right arm behind her knees.

Then he picked her up and spun around with her in his arms.

"Don't!!!," she laughed with a shriek as she hung onto his neck. "You'll injure yourself! I'm not one of those lightweight ballerina types!"

"Nah. I can lift twice your weight," bragged Andy as he stood her back on her feet. "How do you think we Neanderthals carried our women back to our caves?"

"I thought you dragged them by the hair," grinned Robin, lifting her pony tail. Then she walked to a small restroom in the corner of the room. Without closing the door, she splashed water on her face, dried it with a paper towel, and washed her hands before returning to Andy, who was responding to her comment.

"Oh, if you'd ever been to the place where Glacier Pete was found, you'd know that it's not a good place for dragging anyone. It's pretty rocky there."

"Speaking of the cave man thing, how do you think we should handle that?" asked Robin quite seriously. "I'm new to this stuff."

"I think our best bet will be to just embrace it," said Andy. "We'll go to Halloween parties dressed as Fred and Wilma Flintstone."

"I can do that! I can put red coloring in my hair and pull it up in a bun!" giggled Robin as she lifted her ponytail again and rolled it into a bun in her hands.

Andy put his arms around her waist.

And this time, he did kiss her.

They happened to be standing in front of a window, and Gordon and Sunny were watching from the office. "Guess I'd better get back to my sewing room," said Sunny.

"Would it do me any good to ask what you're working on?" asked Gordon.

"Nope."

# CHAPTER 30: FORGING AHEAD

Beth and I heard a lot about that kiss. Of course, at the time, it was spoken in confidence, but since then Robin and Andy have given us permission to put it into their story. Robin told Beth that she'd never really been very impressed with kisses. In her experience, they were usually wet, sloppy, face-mushing events. But Andy's kiss was different. It was warm and sincere. And there was something about his kind, muscular embrace that was perfectly natural and yet strangely exciting.

And all of that came as somewhat of a surprise to Robin. She hadn't expected to feel that from Andy, and felt a bit embarrassed to have underestimated him. I told her she'd have to get in line at the confessional booth, because we've all committed the sin of underestimating Andy at one time or another.

As for Andy himself, he told me that he hadn't been thinking about how the kiss should be done. He was only thinking that the most amazing young woman he had ever met was in front of him and just needed to be loved. And that, of course, is precisely how it should be done. The fact that he, too, felt that excitement all the way to his toes, surprised him as much as anyone else.

~~~

After that evening, I doubt that Andy and Robin found much time for kissing. Leaf removal season was in full operation and it slows for no one. In the forested areas the leaves could be left where they fell, but on the lawns, gardens, campsites, and parking areas, they had to be removed. It's a process involving enormous blowers and vacuums, so it works best if it's done before the leaves get soggy, which sometimes happens within a few days. Or a few minutes.

And when they weren't working at the park, Robin and Andy were going through the process of assuming custody of Dawn's children. It was a delicate and confusing process of balancing Dawn's needs, the children's needs, Robin's needs, and the legal requirements of the custody system.

The physical transfer of the children would be a gradual process. The plan was that the kids would visit "Aunt Robin" frequently, eventually reaching a point where Robin's home would be their primary residence, with visits to or from their mother whenever she was able. Cabin 3 would be cleaned and upgraded for Dawn and Starlight's visits, although they wouldn't be able to stay very long because Dawn needed to stay close to her medical clinic, and Star had a home and responsibilities on the reserve. Andy was glad he hadn't signed up for any classes this semester, because he was going to be pretty busy driving kids back and forth.

Gordon's promotion would be keeping him on the road a lot, so he and Sunny agreed to swap homes with Robin. Cabin 1 would be upgraded for them, and Robin would be moving into the large house where her parents had lived for the last 20 years. She wondered whether Dawn's children would be able to grow up in that house as she had. But it also meant that in the middle of everything else, there would be a lot of packing and cleaning and unpacking to be done.

~~~

When it came time to sign the custody papers, Dawn had relapsed and was back in the hospital. Just before she left her house, she called in a notary and signed the papers. The original papers had listed only Robin as the person receiving custody, but in the line below, Dawn scribbled "and Andy." She didn't know Andy's last name, and didn't have time to find out, so it was the best she could do at the time. Then she had the notary initial it and mail the documents to the custody attorney's office in Sudbury.

The attorney wasn't pleased. Actually, he was a grumpy fellow who was rarely pleased with anyone or anything. It frustrated him when people were careless with their paperwork, and frustrated him even more when people had the bad manners to die or become comatose before the paperwork was completed. So, as Robin and Andy sat across the desk from him, Robin thought him to be one of the most intimidating men she had ever met. He read Dawn's scribbled notes and grumbled, "I don't like this a bit."

"I presume you are Andy?" he grunted.

"Yes, Sir. My full name is Andrew James Neill. I have my birth certificate and Social Security and SIN numbers if you want them." Andy had tried to be prepared for this appointment, including his appearance. He was wearing a crisp button-down shirt, and his hat, which he only took off for serious situations, rested in his lap. But he knew nothing would spare him from the next question.

"And that means you're the Neanderthal guy that I've been hearing about?"

Robin started to open her mouth to object, but Andy was accustomed to this. "Yes, Sir," he replied again.

"Are you two married?"

"No, Sir," answered Andy.

"Why not?" asked the attorney with a growl.

Robin couldn't believe he was asking such questions, but she answered, "Our relationship is fairly new, Sir."

"So you barely know the guy," groaned the attorney.

"Oh, no, we've worked closely together for a year and a half," Robin explained, knowing that it wasn't going to satisfy this man.

"Well, all I know is that Dawn didn't know him well enough even to write his full name. And every time I talk with her, she's in and out of the hospital and not sure whether she's going to survive or not," the grumpy attorney said, throwing up his hands as if this was something people did for the express purpose of making his life difficult.

Composing himself a bit, Grumpy looked at Robin and said, "Your position on this document is fairly secure. It has all the necessary information, and, more importantly, you are a blood relative. You had known the children and even been a godparent to them since they were born."

Robin nodded. Actually, she'd only seen the kids two or three times a year, but she wasn't about to bring that up now.

Then Grumpy turned to Andy. "You, not so much. You only met the parents once. You're not related, and you have no legal connection to the family other than as an employee. You have dual citizenship but you've spent most of your life in the United States. And then there's this whole issue of you being actually a different species."

Grumpy leaned back in his chair and continued. "As long as Dawn survives, and Robin remains in good health, it's unlikely that there will be a problem. But if anything happens to either of them, even temporarily, this document might not hold up. You could put your heart and soul into these kids and then have them ripped out from under you." He sighed in a way that showed some compassion underneath all that bluster.

"I've seen it happen in cases much less complicated than yours."

"How would marriage change any of that?" asked Robin.

"Andrew would become a legal member of your family, as well as your legal spouse, with all the rights and responsibilities that accompany that role," answered Grumpy, adding, "Too many young people these days don't bother to get married, and they don't realize the legal implications."

Then he explained the paperwork to Robin and Andy, got their signatures, and said he would call them in two weeks. "Meanwhile," he said, "keep doing what you're doing as far as getting the kids acclimated, and good luck to both of you. You'll need it."

As Robin and Andy left, they heard him reading the signatures and mumbling, "Her address at the park is 'Cabin 1' and his is 'Cabin 2?' Oh, Heaven help me."

# CHAPTER 3I: THE QUESTIONS

Okay, this is Larry again. When Andy called me by Skype a few days later, he seemed baffled by Robin's response to the attorney session. He told me that she had said nothing more about their relationship. Instead, she focused on organizing and completing the work at home and in the park. She packed up her parents' household items and her own for their upcoming household swap, communicated with Dawn's mother about the kids, scheduled a visit for the following week, and worked with Andy on the usual autumn projects at the park.

"That attorney literally scolded us about not being married, and yet she hasn't even mentioned it since then. When she hugs me, she hangs on as if she never wants to let go, but not a word about the future of our relationship," Andy said.

"Do you *want* to marry her?" I asked. "I mean, in absolute seriousness, considering all the responsibilities involved, do – you – want – to – marry – her?"

"Oh, I've given it a lot of thought, and yes, I do want to marry her," replied Andy. "But she's the one who's up to her ears in responsibilities, trying to keep her situation under control, and she hasn't even suggested it."

"That's my whole point," I explained. "She IS the person in control of the situation, which is precisely why she can't be the one to initiate this discussion. It would be an abuse of power. For starters, you are only 19 years old…"

"Actually, three months short of 20," interrupted Andy, suddenly realizing that he felt as if he had aged about five years in the last two years.

"Okay, almost 20, but she's still a year and a half older than you," I continued, "and that's only one of the ways in which the balance of power is tipped in her favor."

I held up my fingers to the screen and started counting on them. "Let's see… she's a year farther along in her education… more experienced in relationships and in her profession… intellectually advanced… the boss's daughter… and starting next spring she's literally going to be your boss. And that imbalance isn't going to change anytime soon."

I removed my fingers from view, but I was still counting and wondering how I suddenly became so obsessed with math. "This means two things for you. First, it means that you need to decide whether you're okay with that imbalance."

Andy nodded, and I continued. "Second, it means that she could get into a ton of trouble for misusing that power. She has already stuck her neck out declaring that she loves you. If there was any implication that she pressured you into marrying her, she could lose everything she's worked for. Or her hesitancy might be more about protecting you than herself. She probably doesn't want to pressure you into a commitment that you could regret later."

Andy took it all in. "So, I'm going to have to be the one to ask," he said resolutely.

"If you're sure that's what you want, then yes," I said. "And here's something else that I've learned throughout the years. When a courtship process is accelerated, there are going to be a lot of questions to be answered, so don't try to skip over them. Some couples get married after years of living together, so the questions have already been answered, but that's not the case for you two. I'm guessing you haven't even shared a mattress yet?"

Andy shook his head. "No, not even close. The chemistry is definitely there, but it's been carefully controlled. We don't enter each other's cabins."

"And that's perfectly appropriate," I said. "But it means that the pillow talk and long conversations on the sofa haven't happened, so learning the details about each other will have to be a deliberate and scheduled process, similar to a job interview."

Andy nodded. "That's good. Robin likes things to be deliberate and scheduled."

"And maybe you'd better start by finding out her ring size," I added.

After our call ended, Beth walked into the room and sat beside me, having heard all of it. "How do I get myself into these things?" I groaned as I grasped her hand. "How did Lamebrain get in the position of trying to be a pre-nuptial counselor?"

"Oh, I think you know how you got here," she laughed, squeezing my hand. "But your Lamebrain days were a long time ago. You're doing just fine."

Meanwhile, Andy called his mother.

# CHAPTER 32: THE ANSWERS

Three days later, Andy asked Robin to meet him in the nature center at the end of the day. When she arrived, he was sitting on that same bench where they had talked three weeks earlier. It was November and the heaters weren't turned on, so they were both wearing their jackets. Andy had an unusually serious look on his face. "This will only take a couple of minutes," he said, "but I need you to let me speak before you jump to any conclusions."

Robin nodded, wondering what he was up to. Usually, it would be something funny, but she could tell that today would be different. Besides, his hat was sitting on the bench beside him.

He asked, "Are you free tomorrow evening after supper? Maybe around 7 p.m.?"

"Yes, unless something unexpected comes up," she answered. It seemed as if unexpected things were coming up often these days.

"Good," Andy said, still very serious in his tone. "Because now it's my turn to say, 'we need to talk.' I'd like you to meet me here tomorrow evening for a conversation – just a conversation – about marriage. If your part of the conversation is to say that you would never consider it, or that you would never consider it with me, then we'll know that, and we'll work with it."

He took a deep breath. "This is going to require some preparation, which is why I'm not asking to discuss it tonight. I'll bring the dessert, and some tea, and we'll both bring lists of *all* the things we want to talk about." He made a sweeping gesture. "Nothing will be off the table. We'll talk about ourselves, and we'll ask questions of each other."

"It will be like a job interview," he continued. "At the end of the conversation, if either of us decides that we don't want the job, then at least we can stop beating around the bush. We'll know what we have and what we don't have.

Do you have any questions?"

"Uh, no," answered Robin.

"Great!" said Andy, with a smile that was businesslike, or at least as businesslike as a Neanderthal face can look. "I'll see you tomorrow. And if one session isn't enough, we'll schedule more," he said as he picked up his hat.

He escorted her out and locked the door behind them. "Oh, if you open this building for any reason tomorrow, be sure to lock it when you leave," he said. "I've got an antique item stored in the drawer under the showcase." Robin nodded, and Andy left.

It was Robin's turn to be confused. She had heard Andy describe himself as "a determined little boy," and she had seen it in his work at the park, but this was the first time she'd seen that determination in a personal setting. She was glad he was capable of pulling this situation together, but a bit sorry that he had to.

In reality, Andy's stomach had been tied in knots throughout his little speech, and as soon as it was over he ran to his cabin to grab his bottle of Tums and to call and tell me about it. His voice was shaking, but he was relieved that he had gotten it over with. By tomorrow evening, for better or worse, he would have some idea where he stood.

~~~

When they met the next evening, Andy had built a fire in the fireplace, and he brought seat cushions and lap blankets for the two Adirondack chairs that he had set up facing the fireplace. Between the chairs he had set up two small side tables with hot tea and blueberry muffins that he had just baked from blueberries that he'd picked earlier in the season.

And, of course, he brought lists, and so did Robin. Each of them talked about their past and their plans for the future, about their beliefs regarding raising children, about their finances and career goals, about religion and politics, about their emotional pain and what made them happy or angry. They talked about how they thought disputes should be settled, how work should be distributed, how money should be handled, and what vacations or retirement would look like. The muffins disappeared, and the teapot was refilled and reheated in the fireplace twice. They even took a couple of bathroom breaks.

And when they were done, Andy took a small box from the drawer under the showcase. Leaving his hat on top of the showcase, he walked to Robin's chair and got down on one knee.

# CHAPTER 33: THE ARRANGEMENTS

"It belonged to his great grandmother. It's over 80 years old!" Robin told her parents as she extended her left arm and showed them the ring. Then she took a deep breath and asked them whether they were okay with her engagement, although she told me later that she wasn't sure what she would have done if they weren't. Fortunately, it wasn't a problem. They had known she was in love with Andy before she knew it, or at least before she admitted it to herself.

"I'm the guy who hired him, remember?" pointed out Gordon with a smile. "I knew there was something special about Andy back then, although I didn't know I was hiring him for the position of son-in-law. I believe he will treat you well, and that's what a father wants for his daughter."

"Have you decided yet when you're going to get married?" asked Sunny.

"Yes, I want to talk with you about that," replied Robin. "Because of the child custody situation, we don't want to wait until summer, so I'm thinking of Christmas Eve. Unfortunately, Andy's family won't be able to attend in person due to COVID restrictions, so we'll include them by video.

"But for our family, I'd like to invite Dawn and her kids and Starlight to stay here for the holiday. Andy would pick them up, and we could do all the meal preparations and clean-up, so Dawn and her mom wouldn't have to exhaust themselves with it. It will also give me and Andy some time to get to know the kids."

Sunny and Gordon looked at each other and nodded. "As usual, my daughter has come up with an excellent solution," bragged Gordon. "I'm proud of the way you take everyone into consideration. I hope Andy appreciates you."

"Oh, he does, Dad. You know he does."

"The Christmas suggestion works fine for me, if Dawn agrees," said Sunny. "Have you given any thought to what you'd like to wear for the wedding?"

"Not yet," answered Robin. "I have a blue skirt that should work."

"Well, I have another option for you to consider," Sunny continued. She led Robin into the sewing room, with Gordon following close behind. Then Sunny reached into the closet and pulled out the dress that she had been working on so diligently.

"Mom, you *made* this? For *me*?" gasped Robin. "It's beautiful! You're beautiful!" and she kissed her mother on the cheek.

Not every girl would want her mother to select her wedding gown, but you had to know Robin and Sunny to understand why this works. Robin is a very practical person who generally tries to focus on just getting the job done. Her mother has an artistic streak and a level of patience for craftsmanship that Robin has always appreciated, and never more than at that moment.

Robin described the dress as a simple A-line gown made of white cotton eyelet, which is one of Robin's favorite fabrics, with a separate white cotton liner. It had a scoop neckline with a scalloped edge, and sleeves that stopped a few inches above the elbow. At the end of those sleeves, Sunny had crocheted an extension of scalloped lace. Sunny knew her daughter's shape and preferences, and had taken all of it into consideration when she created this dress. The side seams were only loosely hand-stitched with plenty of extra fabric so that the dress could be fitted easily when the time was right.

"If you decide to wear the dress, you have a couple of options," added Sunny. "If you want to wear it as is, that's fine. If you want to add a Native flair, I have this," and she brought out a colorful hand-beaded sash to be worn around the waist. "And I have extra beads, so we can add a few into the lace sleeves for accent."

Robin shook her head slowly, and for a moment Sunny thought Robin was declining the beads, but that wasn't the intent at all. Robin was just overwhelmed by the amount of care and detail that her mother had put into this work. Regaining her composure, Robin replied, "Yes, definitely the beaded sash, and the additional beads on the sleeves, too, if it's not too much trouble."

"I haven't hemmed up the dress yet because I didn't know what length you'd want," continued Sunny.

"Gosh, I don't know. We're planning to get married in front of the stone fireplace in the nature center, so maybe leave it long? Just above my shoes?" suggested Robin.

"Oh, shoes! I almost forgot," exclaimed Sunny, reaching for a box on the closet shelf.

"You thought of that, too? Yes, of course you did," added Robin with an eye-roll.

The shoes were made from a pair of wedge sandals that Robin had thrown in the trash at the end of the summer after the straps broke. Sunny had fished them out, cut away the broken straps, and replaced them with crocheted uppers and ankle straps.

"I was afraid if I didn't, you'd wear your athletic shoes or work boots," grinned Sunny.

"Good call," answered Robin with a laugh.

Later that day, when Robin told Andy about the dress (without going into too much detail to avoid spoiling the surprise) his response was, "That's great! So what do you think I should wear?"

"Well, I don't know what the typical Neanderthal wedding costume would be, so wear whatever you want," quipped Robin.

"Whatever I wear, it will probably have to be something that my mom sends from Michigan, because I didn't bring any dress-up clothes here," Andy said.

Robin nodded and said, "Okay, just have your mom call my mom and they'll figure it out."

"Works for me," concluded Andy.

# CHAPTER 34: ONWARD TOGETHER

Weddings can be a lot of different things: serious or silly, traditional or eclectic, conservative or corny. Andy and Robin's wedding was a little of everything. Well, everything except stuffy. It definitely wasn't that.

For Sunny, who could create amazing things from almost nothing, decorations were a top priority. She draped the stone fireplace in a garland of pine and cedar branches, trimmed it with tiny white lights, and placed red bows with white chrysanthemums at the peaks of the loops. Above the fireplace, she hung a huge wreath made from spruce and white flowers, with little lace angels on both sides and wedding bells at the top. She placed nine white candles on the mantle, while potted mums and poinsettias rested on the floor.

A low fire burned in the fireplace as Andy and Robin faced each other. Robin's bouquet, also arranged by Sunny, was made of red roses and white mums with sprigs of spruce, cedar and bright red winterberries. Robin wore a silver chain necklace sent to her by Alicia, and her long black hair hung in two braids over the front of her white dress, stopping just short of the beaded sash. Her headpiece was made of tiny white flowers, and at the last minute, Sunny had attached a veil to the back of it, made from a piece of mosquito netting that had ripped off of an old tent. "I had to try a few things to get it white," smiled Sunny.

*Creating Andy*

Andy's wide smile has always been one of his defining features, but I'd never seen it as big as when he stood facing his bride. He wore what his mother and Aiden had sent him: black dress pants, a grey-and-white pin-striped shirt, black tie, and a brand new black narrow-brimmed hat, just to be festive. He had poked a small white mum into the side of the hat band, and he wore a rose boutonniere on his pocket.

Little Kyle, now almost four years old, handed them the rings and then climbed into Gordon's lap, where he held a plush woolly mammoth toy that Andy had given him.

As Andy and Robin exchanged their vows, Sunny clasped hands with Gordon on her right and Starlight on her left. Starlight was using her other hand to pet her little dog, Lulu, who rested in her lap. Dawn, in her wheelchair with her oxygen concentrator humming, sat on the other side of Starlight with Kayla in her lap. When Kayla began to fuss, Dawn nursed her, just as another mother may have done in Bethlehem two thousand years earlier, and as Glacier Pete's mother undoubtedly did thousands of years before that, and countless other mothers in between. Recorded soft music played in the background, and there was peace.

A few minutes later, when the minister pronounced them husband and wife, the peace gave way to cheers, and Andy pretty much exploded with joy. He again picked up Robin and whirled her around.

After he stood her back on her feet, he pumped his fists, did a little stomping dance with his feet and yelled, "Eeee-yesss!!!" as the guests laughed.

"Chill, Cave Man!" grinned Robin, as everyone laughed again. Then she directed the guests to the food tables, where Andy and Robin giggled their way through the cake-cutting ritual. After everyone had eaten, Andy picked up his guitar. He couldn't sing, but Robin and some of the guests did, so they joined for an odd blend of Christmas carols, love songs, and folk melodies.

Outside, snow fell steadily. Late the next day, Andy would begin his winter job driving a snowplow truck, but, for now, it was just family and a few neighbors and friends joined in celebration.

Although I could see every detail of that day's event, I couldn't be there in person. Andy's family also had to watch from home, but Aiden and I helped Arnie and Alicia set up a large screen for viewing and a video camera for participating. In Ontario, a video-tech student who had worked at the park that summer returned to the nature center and set up multiple cameras from various angles. He also set up a wide screen on the groom's side of the aisle, so Andy could see his family during the ceremony. Louis and Beth and I were on the screen, too, appearing by zoom from our respective homes.

After the ceremony, Andy stopped by the screen to chat with his family. When he left to help at the food table, Beth and I visited with Alicia and Arnie on the zoom screen. Arnie put his arm around Alicia's shoulder and said, "Well, I guess we did it. Andy's on his own now."

Alicia replied, "Yes, we did. I'm still not sure *how* we did it, but we did it."

I added, "I'm not sure how you did it, either, but I'm grateful that you did. Thank you."

"You're welcome," laughed Arnie, "but you still owe me, big time."

"Oh, I'm very much aware of that," I answered with a grin.

"No, he doesn't!" Alicia said to Arnie, and then turned to face me. "I'm convinced that Andy was meant to be here, and I declare you officially off the hook," she said with a wide gesture.

I bowed ceremoniously, Arnie scowled comically, and we all laughed.

~~~

The following summer, the Canadian border opened up, and the three cottages on the Magnetawan got plenty of use as Arnie and Alicia, and sometimes Aiden and his new companion, Paul, came to spend time with the new family. Beth and I and the girls got to use one of the cottages for a couple of weeks, too.

Arnie and Alicia sold Ivy House back to the university and purchased a house on 16 acres outside of town. They no longer needed assistance from the university staff, so a home that offered seclusion and natural surroundings would work better for them and for Andy's new family during visits.

Just two decades earlier, none of us had known whether Andy could, or even should, survive. We didn't know whether he would ever speak or read or find his path in this crazy modern world that we live in. Yet here he was, surprising us all again, as he had done so many times since the day he was born. He had a productive life. He had purpose. And now he had someone to share it with.

We knew that Andy's new life with Robin would not always be easy. Kyle and Kayla had lost their father, and their mother would be at best a sporadic figure in their lives. But Andy and Robin were up to the challenge. They would share their love and their energy and their park in the wilderness to give these kids every chance at life, just as their parents had done for them.

And as their ancestors had done forty thousand years ago.

~~~

**THE END**

# CLAIMS AND DISCLAIMERS
# BY THE AUTHOR

First, the obvious: All characters in this story are fictional. Any resemblance to persons living or dead is purely coincidental.

Glacier Pete, and the location in which he was found, Glacier Peaks, are fictional.

I'm not an expert on Neanderthals, although I'm fascinated with the subject. To the best of my limited research, the facts about Neanderthals presented in this story are reasonably accurate. If you have any questions about them, you probably know how to use Google.

I also did a limited amount of research about cloning, but keep in mind that this is science-fiction, with the emphasis on fiction. (If we're going to clone anything extinct, let's start with the Passenger Pigeon.)

The places and events in this story are a mixed bag of fact and fiction:

Pine State University and its accompanying reproductive clinic are completely fictional.

Michigan State University is real, and it does have programs for forestry and horticulture. I attended that college as a horticulture student and took many of the classes mentioned in the story.

The "Magic Tree House Facts" books and the "I Survived" books for 2nd and 3rd graders are real and were suggested for my story by a friend who raised kids during the same time frame as the fictional Andy.

The incident in which a biology teacher takes his 10th grade students out to prune pine trees actually happened to me when I was in high school, and set me on my course to horticulture. I also worked for a parks department, although not the ones mentioned in the story.

The Magnetawan River in Ontario is real. My grandfather had a cottage on that river near Britt. I was too young to remember anything except that the river banks had big boulders and there were wild blueberries growing near the cottage.

Sudbury, Ontario is real, but I've never been there and I know very little about it.

Ontario has some excellent provincial parks, but the one in my story is strictly fictional.

I know nothing about child custody laws and sincerely doubt that it would matter whether the couple receiving custody was married or not. Then again, I don't know any couples in which one partner is Neanderthal.

Made in the USA
Coppell, TX
01 November 2022

85548969R00105